# A SORT OF PEACE

*Also by* Margaret Thomson Davis

THE BREADMAKERS
A BABY MIGHT BE CRYING

# A SORT OF PEACE

*by*

# Margaret Thomson Davis

**Allison & Busby**
published by W. H. Allen & Co. Plc

An Allison & Busby book
Published by
W. H. Allen & Co. Plc
44 Hill Street
London W1X 8LB

First published in Great Britain
by Allison & Busby 1973

Reprinted May 1988

Printed and bound in Great Britain by
Adlard & Son Ltd, The Garden City Press
Letchworth, Herts

ISBN 0 85031 105 5

The Moving Finger writes; and, having writ,
Moves on: nor all thy Piety nor Wit
Shall lure it back to cancel half a Line,
Nor all thy Tears wash out a Word of it.

*The Rubáiyát of Omar Khayyám*

# Chapter One

Old Duncan MacNair kept more and more to the tiny bedroom allocated to him. There he crouched inside his second-hand, loose-fitting clothes, his boots toeing the fender, his gnarled hands palming close to the heat of the gas fire. There he chewed his dentures and scratched uncomprehendingly at his beard and filled sticky glasses from bottles he kept hidden in the wardrobe.

He had never recovered from the shock of losing his property. He had owned a general grocery and bakery shop with a bakehouse at the back and above three stories of flats and a couple of attics.

He never tired of rambling on about War Damage Premiums and how he was going to rebuild his shop and bakehouse and carry on business as usual. He was over seventy now and Catriona could not see much hope of it happening.

On her way to work each day she passed the place that had once been her home. Her husband Melvin MacNair, old Duncan's son, had been so proud of that flat above the bakery. She remembered how he strutted like a peacock as he showed her round and told her how his first wife had polished the floors, and the doors and even some of the walls until they shone like glass.

"There's not another house in Clydend or even in the whole of Glasgow that could hold a candle to this," he often boasted.

She had been sixteen then, much younger than Melvin and as innocent and unsuspecting as an infant. Only the romantic fairy tales she avidly read and her desperation to escape from her mother's house had made her blurt out a rash "yes" to his sudden proposal of marriage.

Now Melvin was in a prisoner-of-war camp in Germany, and Catriona had capitulated to her mother and moved to her parents' house in Farmbank taking the children and old Duncan with her.

In Farmbank the pale grey uniformity of the houses created their own desolation. It was not very far from Clydend but there the MacNair building had been mellow with age and its tenants and customers spiced with a richness of character that the Farmbank housing scheme lacked.

Travelling to the centre of the city every day she felt magnetised to the right-hand side of the tramcar where she could sit rocking gently to the motion of the tram and gaze out the window, her eyes searching for Dessie Street. The hope never left her that maybe that night three years ago in 1941 had just been a dream. Only in nightmares could things like that happen. Over and over again her mind groped to sort out the facts, like a schoolteacher determined to make a stupid child comprehend. . . .

The sirens go. Everyone in the building troops downstairs to the bakehouse lobby. The bakehouse lobby is warm and safe.

They gossip:

"Did you know Slasher Dawson's home on leave?" somebody says. "A friend of mine in Govan was telling me she saw Slasher sauntering along with a pal when one of these incendiary bombs dropped in front of him. 'Sandbags,' he bawled, and quick as lightning his pal, a wee bachly fella about half the size of Slasher, streaked into the nearest close and came staggering out with sandbags on his back. With a flourish Slasher flicked a razor from his waistcoat pocket, slashed at the sandbags and emptied sand on top of the bomb. It frizzled out, no bother, and he strolled away."

2

Everybody laughs.

They are sitting arms and legs atangle on the lobby floor. Fergus's mattress and Robert's pram are crushed in the middle.

She says, "Look at that wee pet. Wide awake and not a whimper."

She is crouched on the floor close to the pram with her knees hugged under her chin. Her head is leaning to one side as she gazes at her baby. She begins to sing to him. He stares back at her, wide-eyed with love and delight.

> "Wee Willie Winkie
>   Runs through the town,
>   Up stairs and down stairs
>   In his night-gown,
>   Tirling at the window,
>   Crying at the lock,
>   'Are all the weans in their beds,
>   For it's now ten o'clock?'"

There is more singing. Broad Glasgow voices. Somebody leads with the shout, "Everybody together . . ."

"I belong to Glasgow," they sing.

She goes through to the bakehouse to make tea. It is her turn.

They are belting out another song now. Voices are bouncing and swaggering.

> "Just a wee doch and doris,
>   Just a wee yin that's a',
>   Just a wee doch and doris
>   Before ye gang awa' . . ."

She smiles to herself as she sets cups on a tray.

". . . And if you can say, 'It's a braw bricht moonlicht nicht', Yer aw richt, ye ken!"

3

The song screeches to an end in a hurricane of hilarity.

Despite the noise of the laughter she hears a fast, piercing whistle.. . .

Catriona's mind kept stalling with horror at that point. She remembered what happened but the pain of it was too much to bear. Yet she had borne it. She had wept. She had not wept. For long hours she ignored all thought of it. At other times she moaned and nursed herself, and saw Robert's face, eyes beaming adoration up at her, mouth opening in toothless trusting smile.

"I told you so," her mother kept saying. "I told you you ought to have let me keep those children safe with me in Farmbank. God works in strange and mysterious ways, Catriona. I told you you'd be punished and someone you loved taken from you. If you had done what I told you, that poor wee lamb would have been alive today!"

Grief shrank into secret places. Guilt carved terrible wounds.

Now the blue tramcar clanged along the side of the Benlin shipyards, and Catriona's heart raced with hope. Opposite, at the corner of Main Road and Dessie Street, was the MacNair building. Above the shop were her windows with the shiny gold curtains. Inside the glistening promise of the windows had been home, privacy, a place to rest, comfortable chairs, familiar beds, a nice square hall, a kitchen with children's toys strewn about.

Smells from the bakehouse had wafted up the stairs with the warmth, hot spicy gingerbread, juicy meat pie, crispy rolls, crusty new bread smells. They had blended with other aromas from the houses: porridge, chips, bacon, rich Scotch broth, toast burning, milk boiling.

Sounds too: a wireless medley—the jaunty strains of "Peg o' my heart, I love you"; echoes of Alvar Liddell's polite news announcements, his voice like a tranquil river that nothing can disturb.

The bickering of a husband and wife eddying to and fro

in the distance, then hastening louder into whirlpools of anger. Little girls playing with happy concentration:

> "I wouldn't have a lassie-o,
>   A lassie-o,
>   A lassie-o,
>   I wouldn't have a lassie-o,
>   I'd rather have a wee laddie,
>   Laddie, laddie, laddie . . ."

The shock of seeing the now desolate piece of waste ground instead of the familiar tenement building never lost its impact for Catriona.

Every day the tram jangled to a stop opposite. Every day she stared and stared. Then the tram carried her away. As usual she alighted further on at Govan Cross and took the subway from there because it was quicker; she could get out at St Enoch's station and just cross over to Buchanan Street and Morton's, the shop where she worked.

Buchanan Street was one of the greatest business and shopping thoroughfares in the city and a most popular rendezvous of the wealthy. There were some very old established and expensive shops in Buchanan Street and Morton's was one of the oldest. The war and higher-paid jobs in munitions had led to a shortage of staff but there was still a manageress, two elderly "alteration hands" and another saleslady called Julie Gemmell.

Julie was nineteen and up in the clouds about going to marry an Air Force officer. There were so many of these rushed wartime affairs now and they reminded Catriona of her own over-hasty although pre-war marriage. The mere thought of Julie's unsuspecting eagerness distressed Catriona. She had agreed to be Julie's matron-of-honour, as married bridesmaids were called, and she looked ahead to the ceremony with nothing but dread.

Only four years separated them in age, yet Catriona felt so much older and sadder. In outward appearance she

5

could have been taken for younger than Julie: despite childbearing she still had a small, boyish underdeveloped body, and her fair hair and timid hazel eyes were on a level with Julie's shoulder.

Julie came from the Gorbals and had a habit of repeating, in a slightly aggressive tone as if she thought you had not heard her the first time, that she was not in the slightest ashamed of the fact. She would toss her glossy hair and make her pageboy roll spring and bob about, and her eyes would acquire a dangerous green sparkle.

"There's nothing wrong with the Gorbals, you know. Plenty of decent, hardworking folk live there."

Catriona agreed wholeheartedly every time she said it.

Julie's excitement about her romance with Reggie Vincent was embarrassing to watch. Her skin took on a fiery hue as if she ran a temperature when she spoke of him.

"An officer!" In an ecstasy of joy she clapped her hands. "Fancy me going with an RAF officer, Catriona. And he's so well educated and all that. Did I tell you he's been to the university?"

She had, innumerable times before.

"And imagine, just imagine—he comes from Kelvinside!" Julie always laughed then and repeated with a comic roll of the eyes and an exaggerated accent: "Kailvinsaide! Cain yew jast aimaigine me raisaiding in Kailvinsaide, Caitriona?"

Memory splintered Catriona's eyes with pain.

Kelvinside was away at the north-west end of the city along Great Western Road, its elegant crescents and terraces curving up on either side and giving the road an even wider and more splendid appearance. Great Western Road led to Bearsden, with its sprawl of large villas and gardens and trees and high walls.

Catriona had been taken there after the Clydend blitz and been fed burned porridge and soup in the Bearsden town hall. Afterwards, but before her mother came to collect

6

her and hustle her off to Farmbank, she had been given sanctuary in what seemed to be the house of her dreams. Too shocked and dazed, she had not paid much attention at the time. Often since, though, she had remembered the place and been amazed at how it matched her pre-war childish imaginings of the home she would have when she married. Many a time as a young girl curled up in the lumpy bed-settee in Farmbank she had seen that house, felt the comfort of it, the luxurious carpets, the fluffy satin quilts.

She thought of it now. One day she would have another home, she vowed. She would have a home of her own for herself and her children, and it would be like that.

Her husband, Melvin, never came into the picture. She dared not allow his big gorilla body and his bulbous-eyed mustachioed face to harass her mind. Fear had always been the strongest emotion Melvin aroused in her and she had not yet gathered enough courage to confess to him in her letters that the house and business and everything that meant so much to him had gone.

She persuaded herself that it was kinder in his circumstances that he should not know. Surely it must be torment enough for Melvin to be locked up behind barbed wire. He had always been such an active man and so proud of his physical fitness; he never used to miss a day of conscientious practice at his physical jerks, as he called them. That was how she most vividly remembered him, hairy hands gripping wrists, shoulders hunching, muscles rippling and ballooning.

Yet every now and again other memories disturbed her like rumbles of thunder that warned of a coming storm.

The last time he had been home he had come straight from Dunkirk and he had been a strange Melvin, thinner and hollow-eyed and prey to mercurial moods that twisted her fear into panic.

Her thoughts dodged him and other harassments. A protective barricade grew inside her head but its walls were never quite high enough or strong enough and always seemed on the verge of crashing down.

Everyday strain, mostly caused by her mother, heaved at her defences.

Her mother had literally snatched the children away from her and insisted on doing everything for them. At the slightest sign of protest or attempt to have anything to do with the children, her mother would remind Catriona of her sin in causing baby Robert's death. If her father, Robert's namesake, tried to come to her rescue, his wife's tongue would immediately lash him, her face twisted with contempt and bitterness.

"Why are you alive and my baby dead and buried?"

Catriona's angry reply snapped out like a reflex action:

"He wasn't your baby! He was mine!"

"May God in His infinite mercy forgive you!" The retort never varied. "You ought to be ashamed to admit you're a mother. You're not fit to lay claim to the word. What kind of mother were you? What did you do to a poor, helpless, trusting wee infant?"

And so it went on, leaving Catriona drowning in a secret whirlpool of agony.

The shop gave her some respite and sometimes, chattering and laughing with Julie, she forgot to be unhappy. Then something Julie would say about love or marriage would unexpectedly tug the strings of her hidden pain and she could barely keep up the pretence of girlish normality. She just wanted to cry and turn away.

On the Saturday before Julie's wedding, Julie explained all the arrangements. The ceremony was to be on Monday at 3 o'clock in Blythswood Registrar's Office. They were both being allowed the afternoon off work. It was a quiet time and the manageress assured them that she would be able to manage and the alteration hands could always come forward and serve if necessary. Julie was to have the next day off as well so that she could spend some time with her new husband before he went back.

8

"We'll both go straight to the Gorbals from the shop," Julie instructed. "You remember and bring all you need. We'll have a cup of tea and a sandwich or something, and change and then take a taxi to the Registrar's Office." Then she did a little dance and gave a strangled, "Yippee, Reggie, here I come!"

A couple of late shoppers appeared and forced her to stop talking of her plans. They both went to attend to the customers, Catriona shyly, with a timid smile of enquiry, Julie, head tossed high, swooping forward in style, arching pencilled eyebrows.

"Yes, modom?"

Afterwards they said a giggling goodbye at the corner of Argyle Street and St Enoch's Square.

"Reggie's telling his mother tonight and I'm visiting there tomorrow for afternoon tea. Aifternoon tea ait Kailvinsaide, no less!"

"I hope everything goes all right. I hope his mother will like you. You know what mothers can be like."

"Och, I've seen a photo of her. She looks quite a nice wee soul. And don't you worry!" Julie patted her hair and arched her brows and gave a little bouncy wiggle of her hips. "After I get through with myself tonight she'll think I'm the cat's pyjamas. I'm going to clean and polish myself from top to toe. I've got beer in to give myself a special shampoo and all the old curlers are lined up at the ready. And I've bought a new nail buff. I'm even going to polish my toes."

She gave a nonchalant demonstration of buffing her fingernails. "Buffety-buff-buff! I'm telling you, pal, once my future mother-in-law sees me, she won't want to change me for the Queen of England! Don't forget to bring your glad rags to the shop on Monday."

Julie waved gaily as she swung off and disappeared among the jostling Argyle Street crowds.

Catriona's laughter faded. The hand raised to return Julie's wave drifted down. Uneasiness itched her mind.

9

Talk of Julie and Reggie's wedding made her think of her own marriage again. Somehow it had brought Melvin closer.

She trembled as she turned into St Enoch's Square, as if her husband might be waiting for her.

She must tell him about the air-raid. She did not dare pretend any more.

# Chapter Two

"For God's sake, Madge! Have a heart!" Alec Jackson appealed to his wife. "I could go back off this leave and never be seen again."

Madge wrestled with the nightdress over her head while he lay in bed boggling at her nakedness. At last her freckled face popped into view and she wriggled the nightdress down over milky body and brown nipples and curly pubic hair.

"I couldn't be that lucky. Not me! Oh, no, you'll come f——ing back all right."

"Madge!"

He could not get accustomed to Madge using the swear word. On the ship it was used all the time and he never gave it a thought, but to hear it coarsen his wife's mouth shocked him deeply.

Not that Madge had ever been an angel. She could bloody and bugger occasionally and she was never above a bit of violence either. Many a female acquaintance of his had been chased off by a battling Madge, dishing out squashed noses and black eyes. He had been at the receiving end of Madge's fist himself and although his mates back on the ship thought it a howl of a yarn when he told it to them, in actual fact it was no joke. Madge had nearly knocked his teeth out.

Still, she had always remained attractive with it. Big, high-hipped, melon-breasted Madge with her long, lean legs, her toothy grin and candid stare.

Only now was he beginning to notice the change in her.

She had lost the naivety that he had once found so attractive. Sometimes there was a hard twist to her mouth and her eyes could change to ice chips. Perhaps the change was more noticeable because he had not seen her very often these past few years, what with Dunkirk and one or two other places. Join the Navy and see the world, they said. After this lot was over they could keep the world. Give him Glasgow any day and his wee house in Springburn and Madge and the weans.

There could be no escaping the fact, though, she was definitely not the same easy-going big-hearted girl she used to be.

Take sex, for instance. She had never denied him before and certainly never quarrelled as she was doing now about him not having a French Letter.

"The queue was about a mile long, hen," he tried to explain. "I would have missed my train if I'd waited."

"You're not bothered about what I might miss. You've never bothered. I've had six weans and I would have had more by now if the bloody Royal Navy hadn't hauled you off."

"Och, you wouldn't be without one of the weans."

He made the mistake of sounding too sure of himself, even quite jocular. Her bonfire of anger immediately flared up again.

"No!" she bawled. "But I'll make f——ing sure I'll be without any more!"

"I wish you wouldn't use that cuss word, hen." He felt genuinely harrowed. He had always been pretty good-natured himself and he certainly had never laid down the law to Madge before. Anything for a peaceful life and a bit of loving, that was his motto.

This was so unlike her. Granted, she had never been quite the same since she found out about his wee bit non-sense a few years back with her friend Catriona MacNair. Later on too she went a bit wild when she discovered he had made a date to go to the pictures with an old customer of his, Ruth Hunter, who was lodging with Catriona at the time.

It had only happened once with Catriona and it had meant nothing. Surely Madge had forgiven and forgotten that long ago? She was still friendly with Catriona, as far as he knew.

As for Ruth Hunter, he had never as much as touched the girl, worse luck. If he had told Madge once, he had told her a thousand times. Ruth and he had barely seated themselves that night when the cinema was bombed. The whole place had caved in and he had never set eyes on the poor cow again. Alec had been lucky to get out alive. He was about the only one who did.

"Shocks you, does it?" Madge flung back her head and roared with laughter, hands on hips, legs apart, the clinging blue of her nightdress straining.

"I don't like to hear it from you, hen."

She climbed into bed over the top of him like a St Bernard dog with backside high up and knees digging down. He let out a howl as one knee almost ground into his crotch.

"For God's sake, Madge! You nearly denied yourself a lifetime of pleasure."

"You'll have been getting your pleasure, all right." She flapped the blankets energetically and the hot sweet smell of her talcum powder puffed up his nostrils. "Sailors are supposed to have a girl in every port but, if I know you, it'll have been every girl in every port."

So that was it! Poor old Madge was terrified he had not enough to go round, and of course before this leave she had been deprived of it for a long, long time.

He struggled to encircle her with his arm.

"Anyone would think, to hear you, that I had been away on a pleasure tour. Listen, hen, I've been concentrating on one thing and one thing alone—keeping alive. That's the God's truth. I'm telling you, Madge, half the time I'm scared rigid. I keep wishing I was a wee fella—about four feet nothing."

She giggled, and taking advantage of her good humour he slipped his hand between her legs, twitching her night-dress up with stealthy fingers.

"Why four feet?" she wanted to know.

"I'm a hell of a target at six feet, that's why, and not only for Jerry planes and guns. It's our own mob as well."

"Eh? Our own guns try and shoot you?"

Surprise slackened her, and he is in there with his hand right away, caressing the moistness of her, making her quiver and arch and make little absent-minded moans of protest.

"It's officers," he murmured in answer to her question, at the same time wriggling his other arm free to manœuvre her nightdress up above her breasts. They hung to one side, tender-looking with delicate blue veins and coffee-coloured nipples beginning to harden. He tickled them with his tongue in between each word and felt them twitch as if his tongue were electrified.

"When they look for volunteers everybody tries to merge into the background and disappear. I can't. I try, but I stick out like your lovely wee titties!"

"Get off!"

Her words held no conviction. Already she was enjoying herself too much and it made his pleasure twice as keen. His mouth searched with increasing urgency, moving down from her breasts to her abdomen until he was burrowing between her legs, his tongue sword-sharp with passion.

She began to moan and squeal with such abandon he was afraid she might waken the weans and they would come through from the next room.

He did not stop what he was doing but he whispered hoarsely, "Shush, hen, shush!"

But it only made her cry out all the louder:

"Oh, God, Alec, I love you!"

Afterwards, when they were lying quiet and exhausted, she gave a big shuddering sigh and announced unexpectedly:

"I hate you, you rotten big midden!"

He laughed as he reached for a cigarette.

"You hate me to stop, you mean!"

"You don't care a damn about me."

"Madge, you're my wife. There's nobody to beat you in the whole world, hen."

"And you've tried them all."

"Och, now, Madge . . ."

"It was bad enough trying to keep track of you when you were an insurance man and just going around Springburn. Now you're gallivanting all over the globe. God knows where you've been and who you've been with."

"Madge, I keep telling you . . ."

"I know what you keep telling me. You were telling me the same thing when you were sniffing around Catriona MacNair and Ruth Hunter."

"I'll swear on the Bible if you like—I never touched Ruth Hunter. As for Catriona, you know what she's like. She asked for it."

"Asked for it? Don't give me that. She was just a wee lassie. You laid her before she knew what was happening. And her man away in the Army as well. You're lower than a worm, Alec."

"Look, hen, it meant nothing to me, absolutely nothing."

"It meant a lot to her though."

"What? You must be kidding. She's a nut-case. She couldn't love a man if she tried."

"She can have a bloody wean without trying."

"All right! All right! So she had a wean. So I said I was sorry. I've been apologising about that for years. Are you never going to forgive and forget?"

"The wean was killed. In the same raid that killed your mother."

He puffed at his cigarette in silence for a minute.

"I know. Poor wee bastard. She'll have got over it by now, though."

"That shows how much you understand." Her voice

15

cracked with bitterness. "You think you know all about women, Alec, but the truth is you're such a randy bugger you never see past their arses."

He shook his head uncomprehendingly.

"Anybody would think she was your wee sister, the way you go on."

"It's not her. It's you. And me. You've probably given me a wean." Her voice turned into itself, became incredulous, as if she could not believe what she was saying. "Another wean would make seven. Seven! You come here, have your way with me, then you buzz off to enjoy yourself somewhere else. You don't care about how I'm going to manage or how I feel."

He began to get rattled.

"Look, hen, will you get this daft idea out of your head once and for all? This bloody war isn't a picnic organised specially for my benefit so that I can get around and keep supplied with girls. If I thought I'd get away with it, I wouldn't go back. There's nothing I'd like better than to stay right here with you, believe me. You should see the build-up of men and hardware down south. My God, hen, there's going to be a hell of a fight any day now. And I've a horrible sinking feeling they're going to shove me in first!"

She started to laugh, quietly, gently, then louder and louder until she was seesawing between hysterical hilarity and moaning tears.

"Women!" he groaned to himself, but he pulled her into his arms and nursed her like one of his children.

"Shush, hen, shush. It'll be all over one of these days and we'll be able to get back to normal."

"I used to trust you, Alec. I really trusted you. You always said it wasn't your fault—it was just that the women wouldn't leave you alone. And I believed you."

"Well, it was true."

"You were always fighting them off, you said. You didn't want anybody else except me, you said."

16

"Neither I do. Madge!" He cuddled her closer. "I'm just counting the days to when I can come back here to you for good. That's the God's truth, so help me!"

She snuffled and wiped her nose on her nightie.

"I miss Ma as well. She was a good soul, your Ma, and a great help with the weans and the book. God, I get tired at times, Alec. I just had to give up the book. Climbing up and down all them stairs collecting every day fair beat me. I don't how how you used to do it and keep so cheery all the time."

"Don't worry about the book, hen. It couldn't be helped. I'll get fixed up with something when I get out, either with the Co-op or the Prudential."

"I put most of the money straight into the Post Office. I had to dip into a few pounds. The weans were needing so many things and it's not so easy with me not working and sometimes I've to pay extra for things on the black market."

"We'll manage all right."

"As long as I've got you, Alec. I'll murder you if you leave me with all them weans."

"Don't worry!"

"I wouldn't need to worry if you didn't give me anything to worry about. How would you like it if I got off with one of them Yanks?"

He laughed, secure in the knowledge that Madge would never look at another man.

"Which kind? A gum-chewing skinny one with steel-rimmed glasses and cropped hair or a gum-chewing hefty fella with tight trousers and a big bum."

She tried not to laugh.

"They get the girls all right. You should see the gum-chewing girls hanging on to their arms and all the kids running after them shouting, 'Any gum, chum?'"

He had seen the girls. Tarts mostly, with pencilled eyebrows and maroon mouths and hair curling on square-shouldered coats or tucked into ropey hair-nets called snoods. Gripping shoulder-bags, they bounced along on streaky orange-painted legs and clumpy shoes.

He was reminded of an experience with a right hairy he had met up with in Pompey. They had been getting along all right until she disappeared into another room, reappeared carrying a whip that looked like something out of *Mutiny on the Bounty*, and invited him to have a go.

"Our boys hate them," Madge went on.

"The girls?"

She dug an elbow into him with such force he yelped in protest.

"The Yanks, stupid! Because they get all the girls."

"And the Poles, and God knows who else I bet! When I was crushing through the crowds at Central Station I could hardly hear a Glasgow tongue. I'm not surprised our lads are peeved. Outnumbered in their own backyard. Wait until after the war, though. Our turn's coming."

"Not your turn." Madge's voice hardened. "You've had your turn."

"For God's sake! When I said that, I didn't mean . . ."

"You never mean anything you say. I found that out years ago."

"You're not going to start all that again."

"I never started anything. I never let you down. I never told you lies. I never slept with your friends."

He groaned and turned over and tried to escape in sleep. Madge twisted away too, leaving a cold tunnel of air between them.

Depression suddenly knocked the props from under him. For the first time in their married life Alec felt Madge had failed him, somehow let him down. All she seemed to think about was herself. All he had heard since he had arrived home was one petty grievance after another. He hadn't been kidding either when he said this might be his last leave. The whole of the Allied armies, navies and air forces seemed to be massing down south. He was beginning to think the only thing that prevented the British Isles from sinking under the weight of it all was the barrage balloons, important and aloof in the sky like fat cigars.

He felt sick at the thought of repeating the experience of his last visit to the French coast. His number had nearly come up then, not to mention a few times elsewhere. It seemed really tempting providence to have another go.

At the same time, like everybody else, he felt sure that it would be the other chaps that would cop it, not him.

His good spirits surged up as quickly as they had sagged. He rolled over and cuddled into his wife's back. She remained stiff and cold and unresponsive. He slipped his hand between her legs and tickled her. Then, straining his head up he whispered close against her ear in broad Glasgow accent:

"Hullo, therr!!"

# Chapter Three

At last Catriona wrote the letter:

"My dear Melvin,

I've been so worried about whether or not I should tell you all that has happened. I know you must have suffered terribly in all the fighting and then to be captured and held prisoner.

It was only because I couldn't bear to think of you suffering any more that I put off telling you until now. But the war won't last forever and I'm beginning to worry about the shock you would get if you arrived back in Glasgow not knowing.

Melvin, my dear, there have been air-raids here and our place was hit. I told you that wee Robert had died. What I didn't tell you was that he was killed. He and most of the others in the building were killed when Dessie Street was destroyed by bombs.

Your lovely flat has gone, Melvin. And the shop. But I've managed to salvage a few bits and pieces and some of the machinery from the bakehouse is still all right and in storage.

Please try not to get too upset, dear. Da is very keen to buy another business and as soon as this terrible war is over and you are home again we'll be able to start afresh.

We'll get another house too, don't worry. Pass the time just now planning how nice you'll make it and all the nice new things you'll have.

You'll understand now why I'm staying with my mother

and father at present. Da is here too, and of course Fergus and Andrew.

Fergus and Andrew are doing well at Farmbank School. Andrew is still in the 'baby class' but Fergus has only about another year to go before he sits his qualifying exam and moves to secondary school.

They send you their love. I'm sure you'd be very proud of them if you saw them setting off to school together each morning. They look so smart in their blazers and caps and white shirts and school ties and both with their school bags on their backs. Andrew is still quite plump and small but Fergus is fairly shooting up. I think he's going to be very tall. He's as thin as ever but very energetic. Andrew has plenty of energy as well and they both love football. I'm afraid when they arrive home each day they don't look smart. Their caps and ties are askew. Their socks are hanging over their shoes. Their shoe-laces are trailing loose behind them. And you should see the filthy state of their faces, their shirts and their knees. Sometimes I get awful angry and rage at them. But then my mother rages at me. I'm afraid she tends to spoil them.

I don't mind telling you, Melvin, I'll be glad when we get another house. Things haven't been too easy for me either. But I mustn't complain. You're worse off than me— away in a strange land and a prisoner. At least I'm getting on fine at my job and saving my wages as hard as I can so we'll be all right for money. I didn't even buy anything new for Julie's wedding.

Julie is the girl I work with. She lives in the Gorbals and is getting married on Monday to an RAF officer from Kelvinside. I'm to be matron-of-honour.

I'd better sign off now, Melvin, as I promised Mummy I'd scrub the bathroom and kitchenette floors. It's about the only thing she'll allow me to do. I mean, she insists on doing everything for the children, even washes and irons their clothes in case I don't do it right.

I get so annoyed with her at times but it doesn't matter

what I say, she talks me down and goes on doing exactly what she wants to. Honestly, Melvin, I do try. The other night she decided to take the boys with her to visit a friend. She'd had them out with her the night before as well and I had visions of them becoming so tired they'd be falling asleep at school the next day.

I said they weren't to go, but of course they wanted to go. They love their gran because she lets them stay up late and spends all her sweets coupons on them. My father's about as bad. He gives them bags of chips in bed and tells them ghost stories and then they're up half the night—Fergus with nightmares and Andrew with indigestion.

But as I was telling you, the other night Mummy was taking them out again and when she refused to listen to me I tried to physically restrain her from taking them out of the house. I mean I actually got a hold of the boys and started pulling them back into the sitting-room, but what with them struggling and my mother punching at me I had to let go before I was half-way along the lobby.

I really don't know what can be done with somebody like my mother. I've never known of anyone with such a strong personality. And yet sometimes I wonder about her strength. She seems to need people so much, it's almost as if she's afraid to be on her own. Maybe all that iron determination hides a very lonely and unhappy person underneath. Anyway she's happy just now with the children here. But I was wondering, Melvin, if I shouldn't be looking around for a wee temporary place. I'd have enough for a deposit and of course I'd keep working and what Da would pay me for his food and board would help.

I don't want to hurt my mother and I feel guilty about leaving her but at the same time I don't know if I can stand it much longer here.

For one thing, there really isn't room. As you know there's just one small bedroom and your da has that. Remember the sitting-room and the bed-settee where I used to sleep before I was married—well, Mummy and

Daddy have that now and the boys have a mattress on the floor beside it. I'm on the sofa in the living-room, jammed up against that big old-fashioned table and wooden chairs. I used to think sleeping on that lumpy settee in the sitting-room was bad enough but at least it made down into a bed. This horsehair sofa is too short even for me and so narrow I'm afraid to turn in case I fall off during the night. Mummy rams the chairs and the table up against it to stop me falling out.

Talk about being in a prison. Every night I'm jammed in there and peering out through the bars of the chairs watching Mummy striding about as happy as a lark, getting the boys' clothes and everything organised for the morning.

Sometimes she sets the table for breakfast and one night the breadknife was lying on the table within my reach and, Melvin, I know this is wicked, and I pray that God will forgive me, but a terrible feeling came over me.

I was lying there very quiet and still, just watching Mummy striding about and singing to herself and folding the boys' clothes, and suddenly this terrible feeling came over me. I wanted to grab that breadknife and plunge it into my mother again and again. Just for a minute the temptation was almost overwhelming. I was frightened at myself, Melvin.

It made me remember poor Sarah that time in Dessie Street when she stabbed her mother-in-law to death. Maybe that was what she felt. I'm frightened in case that feeling comes over me again. I think I'd better look around and try to find some wee place. We can get a bigger, better house after you come home.

I said ages ago that I'd better sign off and here I am, pages later, still writing. I seem to have got quite carried away. It's just that it's so frustrating living at Farmbank like this and there's no one I feel I can talk to about it.

Poor Madge has troubles enough of her own with all that crowd of children in a wee room and kitchen in Springburn. They haven't even an inside toilet.

My friend, Julie—that's the girl I told you about, the one I work with who's getting married on Monday—she's so happy at the prospect of her marriage to her marvellous Reggie she's blissfully unaware of anything or anybody else.

I hope everything goes well for her. I wouldn't like to see her get hurt. I don't know why, but I worry about Julie a lot. I try to feel happy for her but instead I just feel sad. I can't help it. I wish I wasn't going to the wedding.

Honestly, I'm dreading Monday. I know it sounds stupid but even the thought of it depresses me.

Now I feel guilty as well at writing all this to you and making it such a morbid letter.

But of course it couldn't be a cheerful one when its purpose was to tell you about the air-raid.

I know how you'll feel, Melvin, and I'm so very sorry about the house and everything but it wasn't my fault. There was nothing I could do.

Just try to think about the lovely new house you'll have and all the nice things you'll put in it and I'll keep everything all beautifully clean and polished just the way you like it, I promise.

You've always been a strong man, Melvin, and I know you'll be able to weather this bad news and get over it and start planning for the future like I've said.

If your Da can do it—you can do it.

Please try not to worry. Everything will work out all right."

She signed the letter, folded it, put it in an envelope and carefully printed the address.

The house was quiet and empty. Her father was out at the pub. Her mother had taken the boys to the pictures.

Catriona gazed bleakly around at the outsize furniture, dark relics of the Victorian age which had once belonged to her grandparents.

Melvin had often said that it was a disgrace, the way it

24

had been ruined. The table was scratched and burned and ring-marks overlapped in a maze of patterns.

A handle was missing from one of the sideboard doors and it kept squeaking open to reveal a higgledy-piggledy assortment of cups and saucers and plates, a sticky jar of jam, a piece of margarine on a saucer, a jug of milk and a bowl of sugar.

A bulge of damp dross in the grate occasionally spat out bluish flames or puffed black smoke.

The house in Dessie Street had been warm because of the bakehouse underneath.

Catriona crossed her arms on top of the letter and made a nest for her head. There had been times when she had hated the house in Dessie Street because of the way Melvin made a God of it and bullied her into endless scrubbing and polishing.

Yet she wished she could go there now. She longed to go home, to shut the door behind her, to wheel Robert's pram into the warm kitchen.

"Where's my wee boy?" she always used to say before she lifted him out and dandled him on her knee and took off his blue knitted bonnet and coat. He always smiled hugely, his eyes melting up at her with adoration. She saw him now in the crook of her arm and nursed herself with tense-faced, monotonous anguish.

# Chapter Four

Gorbals! The name exploded in his mother's face like one of the ten thousand pounders Reggie's bomb-aimer dropped from his Lancaster over Berlin.

"Oh, no!" Muriel Vincent allowed her husband Norman to coax her into a chair. "I don't believe it."

"I'm sure if we discuss the matter in a . . ."

"Oh, be quiet." She snipped Norman off, then softened round to her son who seemed far too young to be sporting a thick handlebar moustache: "Reggie, tell me it's not true." Her voice changed again. "It's one of those silly university pranks, isn't it?"

Reggie retreated behind a bravado of laughter.

"Good Lord, the 'Varsity'? I was just a kid then."

"You're only twenty now."

"Twenty-one actually, Mother."

"Only a boy."

She remembered him as a skinny child, trotting jerkily beside her towards his first day at Kelvinside Academy. She remembered his hand twisting in her loving grip. He always had a tantalisingly elusive quality. Something of him kept evading her no matter how she kissed or cuddled. Not that she had been a possessive mother. She was sure she had not. He had led a normal happy life with lots of friends of both sexes. No one could accuse her of trying to keep Reggie to herself, of being selfish, or of not wanting him to get married. Her whole life had been devoted to seeing that he got the best of everything. She had always sacrificed herself for Reggie and she had been delighted when he had shown obvious interest in Sandra Brodie, whose father was one of the partners in the well-known firm of Glasgow solicitors, Ford, Brodie and MacAllister.

The Brodies had a detached villa in Bearsden.

Only a few weeks ago she had been enjoying afternoon tea in Mrs Brodie's elegant lounge and weaving with Mrs Brodie delightful plans for Reggie and Sandra's wedding. Over teacups and sighs they pictured Reggie, tall and dashing in his RAF officer's uniform, and Sandra, beautiful and superior-looking in Brussels lace and sweeping train.

Definitely a superior type of girl, Sandra, and so perfect for Reggie. Such a good background. Bearsden, of course, was *the* district, and Sandra had gone to *the* private school in Bearsden and graduated from there to another fee-paying school off Great Western Road, then on to teachers' training college.

Mr Vincent edged his pipe to one side of his mouth to allow his words to escape from the other.

"I must admit this has come as rather a shock to me too, son. The Brodies. Solid people."

"I know, Father. It's just one of these things!"

"Just one of these things?" Muriel cried out. "How can you sound so casual about ruining your whole life?"

"Oh, come now, Mother. How do you know my life is going to be ruined? You don't know anything about Julie. You haven't even met her yet."

Muriel thought of the book which she had innocently acquired at the local lending library not so long ago. The picture it vividly painted of the Gorbals had left an imprint of horror in her mind.

In sordid, stinking rabbit-warrens of tenements, people who were worse than animals urinated in kitchen sinks, got raging drunk on "Red Biddy" and sprawled in their own vomit. Gorbals women had been depicted as completely immoral and the men apparently roamed the streets in gangs and fought each other with razors. No doubt the inhabitants would not all be like that, but still . . .

27

"The Gorbals!" She shuddered. "Of all places!"

Reggie flushed.

"I thought . . . I was hoping . . . Oh, come on, Mother, be a sport, let her come and stay here."

"Here? In Botanic Crescent?" She refused to believe he could be serious. She patted her finger-waved hair that curled in a spaghetti roll against her pearl earrings. "And her unemployed father as well, I suppose. I can just imagine him popping into your father's bank and asking for a loan!"

"Holding it up, more like," her husband guffawed between comforting sucks of smoke.

"What do you think you're laughing at?" She turned on him, her eyes shocked. "How dare you make a joke of this. How dare you! If you had any backbone you'd do something!"

"Muriel, my dear, what can I do? Under Scottish law Reggie has been free to marry without parental consent since he was sixteen."

"Trust you to talk about the law and remind me of Ford, Brodie and MacAllister's. Reggie might have had a partnership. The Brodie money could have been his too, one day. And the villa in Bearsden."

She began to cry, her sobs rushing away with her while she struggled to catch them and subdue them in her lace-edged handkerchief so that the neighbours would not hear.

She could visualise the peaceful crescent outside, with its elegant sweep of terrace houses, in one of which her mother and her father, the Reverend John Reid, still lived. At this end stood the mellow red-sandstone tenement which Norman and she had occupied since their marriage. Norman could not afford one of the terrace-type houses. They were very large, of course. The flats, although spacious, meant much less work and no one could criticise a close like theirs with its tiled walls and Sunday hush every day of the week and each landing church-like with its stained-glass window, ruby red and royal blue.

They were just in the crescent and no more. Botanic

Crescent looped up off a green houseless part of Kelvin Drive.

Not that there was anything wrong with Kelvin Drive or any of the other Drives or Roads or Gardens in the district. Few districts could compare with Kelvinside for sheer beauty and convenience. After all, they were only ten minutes away from the centre of the city.

But here in this quiet little crescent, so near to the busy Great Western Road, yet separated from it by the Royal Botanical Gardens, the River Kelvin and—immediately across the road—the loop of green grass and trees of the crescent, they were in a secret little backwater, a private place of their own. Here Muriel Vincent had been born and brought up. Here she had taken her doll for its daily outing, crossed the road, swept through the gate, bumped the pram down the steep steps to the Kelvin, paraded with dignity along the banks, stopped occasionally to tidy the pram covers, then returned via the other steps that emerged at the tenement end of the crescent where she now lived.

She belonged here, cushioned with beauty and the sighs of trees and the serenading of birds and the sleepy humming of insects.

The idea of coarse, loud-mouthed people—because she was sure the girl's father would not be her only relation—invading this peace appalled her.

What would the neighbours think?

Her weeping loudened brokenheartedly.

"Mother!"

"Muriel, my dear!"

She clutched at Reggie's hands and clung to them, squeezing them tightly against her cheeks and mouth, cupping the smell of her perfume in his palms.

"I can't sleep at nights." Her eyes widened up at him as she strained to discern his face through her tears.

"All the time you're away, Reggie, I'm sick with fear. Nobody knows but your father. I keep a brave face for outside. I tell them I'm glad you're doing your bit for your country. I tell them I'm proud and I am proud, Reggie. Even though I'm ill with fear at the thought of you flying that bomber. Every night I've gone with you to Germany. Every night I've lain awake watching those German searchlights trying to find you in the sky so that their guns can shoot you down."

"Mother!"

"I have. Oh, yes, I have, Reggie. And I've prayed and prayed and you've always come back safe and I've been grateful. I've always thought one day it's going to be all over and everything's going to be all right and you'll be settled with a nice girl and have a happy life. It's the only thing that's kept me sane."

"You mean the whole world to Mother, Reggie, and she's never let you down. She's worked hard to do her bit for chaps like you when they happen to be in Glasgow. She slaves in that church canteen every spare minute she can."

"I know, Father."

"And I've always kept a brave face for you, Reggie. Have I ever made a fuss like this before when you've come home on leave?"

"No, of course not, Mother."

She struggled to find courage now. She released her hold of his hands.

"All I've ever wanted was for you to be happy and to get the best out of life."

"I know." His voice was weakening with misery until his father suddenly announced:

"I'll go and make a cup of tea."

Immediately Reggie brightened with gratitude.

"Righteo, Father."

"Oh, yes, you do that!" Muriel called bitterly after Norman's retreating figure.

Then in the trap of silence that sprung between them, she wondered how she could reach her son.

Impossible to fathom the Reggie she knew in the setting

of the Gorbals. Impossible that Reggie should have anything to do with a product of such a place.

Kelvinside and the Gorbals, although both districts of Glasgow and their inhabitants all Glaswegians, were surely poles apart. She was reminded of the quotation, "East is east and west is west and never the twain shall meet."

"Wait until you see her, Mother. She's A.1. Absolutely splendid."

"You used to say Sandra was splendid, a really nice girl."

"So she is."

"You've known Sandra for years and she adores you."

"Mother, I'm going to marry Julie before I go back on 'Opps'. I was hoping you'd understand."

"Don't talk about going back," she wailed. "You've only just arrived."

"There's something big building up, Mother. I think it's invasion. We've been giving Jerry hell these past few months. I think it's to soften him up before our troops move across the Channel."

Dabbing at her tears, she shook her head.

"Poor Mr Churchill, he has so much to worry him. I'm beginning to feel that I've more than enough to cope with myself."

"It's because of this, you see. I mean because of me having to go back not knowing when I'll get leave again that ..."

"I still maintain it's not like you at all," she interrupted. "Mrs Brodie said that you told Sandra you didn't think rushed wartime marriages in registry offices were fair to a girl."

"I still don't, actually. Anything could happen to a chap and that's a pretty bad show for the girl he leaves behind."

"Oh." She gave a mirthless laugh. "I suppose the RAF pay good allowances."

"Yes, that's what Julie says."

"Oh, Reggie, Reggie!"

"No, no! She didn't mean it like that! We want to start saving for a house of our own, you see."

"Why isn't she here tonight? Why isn't she telling me it's not like that?"

"Steady on! This was my idea."

"You don't want to rush into marriage, Reggie."

"The way things are, I believe it might have been better to wait. But I'm crazy about Julie and . . ." He flashed her an unexpected grin. "You know how determined women can be. You're quite a strong-minded gal yourself."

"Are you going along to see Nanna and Pappa?"

"Yes, of course."

Just then Norman rattled the tea-trolley into the sunlit high-ceilinged room. He brought it to a halt in front of the chair near the window where she was sitting. The peach china edged with gold took on an extra lustre and became pearlised in the sun.

She noticed with a ripple of irritation that he had cut the home-made fruit loaf too thick. Anyone would think he had never heard of rationing. Not that she grudged Reggie anything. If the loaf had been cut in small pieces he could have taken two. It was just not the done thing to serve large thick slices.

In Bearsden, Mrs Brodie offered her guests the tiniest of sandwiches and pinky-fingers of cake, exactly one of each for each person.

Tucking her handkerchief into the pocket of her dress she proceeded to pour tea from the silver tea-pot. Next to Reggie, the tea-pot was her pride and joy. She would match her silver tea-service with any in Bearsden. The shapely tea-pot and sugar bowl and cream jug were family heirlooms handed down from generation to generation.

"The napkins, Norman." She spoke in the quiet, gentle monotone of the long-suffering. "And the hot water."

Reggie half rose from his seat.

"I don't want anything to eat, Mother."

32

She passed him a cup of tea and a plate with a look of reproach and he sunk back down with the weight of it.

"I wouldn't say anything to Nanna and Pappa about all this, Reggie. Not tonight at least. Let them enjoy your visit for a few hours, all right?"

"I'm not ashamed of Julie. She's a wonderful girl. I'll be proud to have her for my wife."

His father patted his pockets as if to make sure his tobacco was still there.

"It may very well be that she is a nice girl, in her own way. The point is you were already committed, my lad."

"No, I wasn't, Father. The truth is . . ."

"Norman!" Muriel interrupted. "The hot water."

Her eyes jabbed daggers into his before smoothing back to Reggie again.

"Nanna and Pappa will be so glad to see you. They barely caught a glimpse of you the last time you were here. I knew no good would come of you going to that dance-hall in town. I suppose that's where you met her. I know you wanted to show that English RAF friend you had with you around and give him a good time while he was here, but what was wrong with the Bearsden Town Hall? Or your own church, or local tennis club dances? You always enjoyed them before."

"Everything's different now, Mother. The war has mixed us all up."

"Well, it's high time everybody was unmixed and back to normal."

"I doubt if anybody will ever be the same again."

He finished his tea and dabbed at his mouth with his napkin, taking care not to spoil the silky twirl of his moustache.

She watched him, marvelling at his debonair good looks and at the same time cringing inside with a sore heart.

Despite Reggie's tall sinewy body, he would always be to her the same evasive, vulnerable little boy.

She still remembered the time years ago before the war

when she had been whipped away to hospital to have her appendix removed. A tiny startled Reggie had not even kissed her goodbye. Yet he had rapidly developed a dangerously high temperature and such alarming symptoms that he had very soon to be taken to the hospital himself.

It eventually occurred to one of the hospital doctors what the cause of the child's unidentifiable illness might be. By this time her operation was over and she was enjoying the luxury of her private flower-filled room and the chocolates and fruit everyone had brought her.

Norman had decided it was better not to tell her about Reggie. She had never forgiven him for that. Afterwards, she raged at him with quiet persistence to make certain he never made such a stupid mistake again. Her little boy might have died while she was lying there idly flipping through magazines and eating chocolates. Her son had needed her, but it took a young doctor, a man with more perception than Norman, to realise this. He brought Reggie into the private room so that he could be reassured that his mother was all right.

Then he was all right. It was the first time she realised what a passionate child he was and she looked ahead with fear to the time when he might be at another woman's mercy. A cruel, ignorant or insensitive girl could use Reggie's vulnerability to suit her own purpose and make his life a misery.

In two days he would be marrying Julie Gemmell from Gorbals Cross. Tomorrow afternoon he was bringing her to meet them for the first time. At best the girl would probably sit dumb and allow Reggie to do all the talking. The atmosphere would be polite and restrained and in no time at all they would make excuses and leave. Panic began to grow and swish inside her like brooms.

Reggie was on the verge of ruining his life. He did not know anything about Julie Gemmell. How could he? There was not enough time for any of them to find out anything.

If only she could talk to the girl on her own, plead with her, if necessary. Then it suddenly occurred to her that she could. All she needed to do was to take a subway train from Byres Road to Bridge Street. She had sat many times in the subway on her way to the centre of the city, staring idly at the map above the windows opposite, so she was familiar with the route. Across the map snaked the blue River Clyde and the underground railway formed a circle that crossed, or, rather, went underneath the river at two places.

She eyed Reggie and Norman, calculating what their reaction would be to her plan of "bearding the lion in its den"—so to speak.

Their immediate horror, she felt sure, would swamp her intentions and prevent her from moving an inch from her chair. Both her husband and son tended to be over-protective. They had always underestimated her, she felt sure.

She decided that it would, at this stage, be simpler and safer not to discuss the matter with them.

Rising, she gathered the dirty teacups on to the trolley. Norman rose too.

"I'll see to that, my dear."

"No. You go along with Reggie, Norman. I'll follow later."

"I insist you go and powder that pretty little nose of yours."

"Norman," she said evenly. "I have other things to do. I want to follow on later."

"Oh. Oh, very well, my dear. Ready then, son?"

She wheeled the trolley out without daring to look at either of them. Already she was protesting to herself with apprehension.

She heard the front door close and hurried back to peer out of the sitting-room window.

Anyone could see they were father and son. They were both tall, and lean, and fair, and they both had the same crooked smile, but Norman stooped as if his head kept tugging his shoulders forward. His step had slowed and he had lost most of his hair.

Her anxious eyes strained to follow the two men all along the crescent until they disappeared inside one of the terrace houses at the other end. Then she retreated into the bedroom to change into her dusty pink suit and hat and to arrange her fur tippet, a present from her parents, high around her throat. Then she tucked her handbag under her arm and smoothed up the fingers of her gloves.

She decided to cut through the Botanic Gardens. That way was most pleasant and she would not be seen from her mother's house.

The iron gate creaked open and she carefully descended the steep steps to the river bank and the bridge. On the bridge she stopped for a minute to gaze at brown water bulging slowly, and the green mountains of trees on either side, gently swinging and bouncing and dipping down.

She would have liked to stay there enjoying the peace for a few minutes more and then go to join Reggie and Norman at her mother's house. She would have been welcomed into her mother's spacious hall by Jessie, her mother's servant, who would have taken her fur. Jessie had worked for her mother for as far back as she could remember. Over the years she had become silver-haired, rather deaf, and a bit of a hypochondriac, but she could still do a decent day's cleaning and fortunately her age saved her from being called away to the forces or munitions. She just continued serving the family and cleaning the house and trying to ignore the war as if it had never happened.

If only it had never happened. Still, it was really too bad of Reggie. One could not blame everything on the war. He should have had more sense.

She turned away in exasperation and distress, her heels clipping on the bridge, then up the steps at the other side and through the main part of the Botanic Gardens. She emerged from the Queen Margaret Drive entrance, at the corner of Great Western Road.

Great Western Road was busy with traffic. This part especially tended to be difficult to cross because of the intersection of Queen Margaret Drive and Byres Road opposite.

Her fingers tightened round her handbag as she waited until the traffic cleared and she could walk across and make her way down Byres Road. She moved purposefully enough, yet she had a fragile quality that stirred men to help her on to buses and immediately to rise and offer her their seats. Even the colour of her and the texture of her clothes had a delicate perfection.

"Bridge Street, please," she asked at the subway ticket counter. "Thank you."

A wind sucked up from the subway with an earthy smell. It flurried the fur round her throat and her soft rose-coloured suit as she decended and it brought with it a wave of fear.

Yet she knew she could not allow her only son to ruin his life without trying to do something about it.

She drew on the thought for courage as the subway train thundered her away into darkness.

# Chapter Five

History was in the very air of the place. At night it whispered up from the river and drifted through the narrow streets in Scotch mist. During the day it swirled with the dust in the tenement closes. All the time it clung to the old grey walls.

Gorbals was famous for the manufacture of firearms, drums, spinning-wheels, cuckoo-clocks and swords. During the fifteenth and sixteenth centuries it was so celebrated for its sword manufacturing that Gorbals swords were judged to be as good in temper and edge as those made by the famous Andrew Ferrars. Its harquebuses or handguns were equal to those of Ghent, Milan or Paris and by the first quarter of the nineteenth century the only individuals in the west of Scotland who manufactured guns were found in the Gorbals. Gorbals was a busy place, especially during the wars between England and Scotland.

The beginning of the nineteenth century also saw cotton-spinning as one of its principal industries. Since then numerous iron-founding and engineering works had been erected within the old Barony, including the famous Dixon's Blazes that lit the sky over Glasgow like a giant ball of fire.

Julie's father, Dode Gemmell, had been a moulder in one of the foundries. He had sweated his strength away at the furnaces and outside in the cold Scottish winds he had caught chill after chill. The chills became pneumonia and the pneumonia, tuberculosis of the lungs. He had been forced to give up work and for a long time now he had been on the dole.

He wore a checked cloth cap, or "bunnet", and a white muffler instead of a collar and tie, except when Julie had visitors. Then Julie shoved a clean collar at him and said:

"Right, you bachly auld tramp, make yourself respectable or I'll be disowning you!"

"You canni dae that, hen," he'd chortle. "Anybody can see you've got the Gemmell beak!"

He was a good-natured, cheery man despite his sucked-in face and eyes set in dark brown parchment; his gummy grin made no secret of the fact that he had not one tooth in his head. He hawked and coughed a lot and hung about the close or one of the street corners at Gorbals Cross, rubbing his hands and shuffling from one foot to the other. Always eager to plunge into energetic conversation on football or any subject at all, he would jerk his head and give a cheery "Aye!" of greeting to anyone who passed, friend or stranger, it made no difference.

He was proud to belong to the "Red Clyde", a staunch supporter of the Gorbals Labour MP George Buchanan, and an enthusiastic admirer of Jimmy Maxton, the long-haired fiery-eyed member for Bridgeton.

He identified warmly and experienced keen fellow feelings with workers in other districts, towns or countries and his admiration for Soviet Russia knew no bounds.

Ordinary working men in Russia had successfully risen up in revolt against the injustices and indignities that all working men suffered. This knowledge gave Dode's life real hope. He followed the Russians' progress in the war as if they were his much cherished brothers.

At some Red Army victory he would proudly shout to passers-by, "What do you think of Old Joe now, eh?"

He had never been much of a drinker of the "hard stuff" but the moulding had been thirsty work and made a man need a few pints.

No longer fit for work, he still enjoyed his beer and Saturday night in one of the Gorbals Cross pubs had become a ritual. He eagerly looked forward to the arguments about football and politics, among the noisy, sweaty crush of men. He shouted and cursed and laughed with them in the coffin-shaped bar with the sawdust floor and enjoyed the complete lack of restraint that the absence of women afforded.

Sometimes, if his horse came in or if one of his mates won a few bob, there would be whisky as well as beer and he would get a "wee bit fu". He was even cheerier and friendlier in his cups and Julie could never bring herself to be angry with him for long. Although she would punch him on the arm and scold:

"Do you want to disgrace me? You drunken auld rascal. Away through to your bed!"

She never invited any friends to the house on Saturdays. Sunday she considered to be her best day because she had time to prepare everything and also to do a bit of shopping. The whole of Scotland might be as quiet as a grave on Sundays with shops, pubs and all places of entertainment closed and everybody observing the Scottish Sabbath. But in Gorbals it was always different.

Most of Glasgow's large population of Jews at some time or other had lived here. Many still did and most of the small shops and businesses in the area were owned by Jewish families who kept Saturday as their "Shabbos". As a result the Christian Sunday to them meant business as usual, and all the shops did a roaring trade and the Gorbals streets were crowded.

Mrs Goldberg who lived downstairs from Julie was a very orthodox old Jewish lady and her beliefs prevented her from doing anything on her Sabbath, even cooking or lighting a fire. So every Saturday morning before leaving for work, Julie ran in to Mrs Goldberg's house and lit her fire and made her a cup of tea. On the way home she looked in again to see to things and each time the old lady gave her the same greeting.

"A goot voch to you, Julie."

And Julie would laugh and give the Jewish greeting back.

"And a bessern to you, Mrs Goldberg!"

The last visitor to the Gemmells' had been Catriona and she had come on a Sunday. Julie remembered with pride how clean and tidy the house had looked. The tiny room and kitchen flat with the cavity or hole-in-the-wall beds had been so spotless it was practically antiseptic. She had been especially proud of using napkins at tea-time. She had made them from an old tablecloth and they looked really classy. Her only worry had been that her dad would forget what they were for and do something terrible with his, like using it for a hanky.

She knew that the MacNairs were business people and quite well-off but no one, not even a MacNair, was going to be allowed to say that just because the Gemmells came from an old Gorbals tenement they were dirty or ignorant.

She was as good as anybody anywhere and so was her dad and so were their neighbours. It was not their fault that there was not any hot water in their tenement and the lavatories had to be shared and were outside on the landings. In fact, in a cupboard-size room and kitchen with a smoking iron grate, and a lightless lavatory as cold as the North Pole, and only a shoe-box of a sink served by one cold water tap, it was difficult to live decently. It took guts. Those who did keep clean and respectable—and that meant the majority of Gorbals folk—were better, not worse, than people from the so-called better-class districts. Julie believed the people of Gorbals deserved a Victoria Cross.

That Saturday, after leaving Catriona at St Enoch's Square, she swung along, skilfully weaving in and out and roundabout the waves of people that surged along Argyle Street. There was a bounce to her walk and a jiggle of buttocks and breasts and a bounce of hair. It was good to be young and in love and buoyantly alive in dear old Glasgow.

She loved the place almost as much as she loved Reggie.

Sometimes she felt so happy she almost bounced right up in the air and floated along high above the crowds in heady communion with the city.

Dear old, dirty old, friendly old, beautiful old Glasgow!

She could see the Tolbooth at Glasgow Cross now but she turned off to the right before the Cross and went down Stockwell Street towards the river.

Stockwell Street used to have a well called the Ratten Well that was notorious for its impure water, and the Ratten Well featured in the story of how Stockwell Street came by its name. There had been a skirmish there between a small party of Scots led by Wallace and the English, and afterwards the victorious Scots flung the dead English into the Ratten Well to Wallace's cry—"Stock it well, lads, stock it well!"

It had been in Stockwell Street that the wealthy Robert Dreghorn, or Bob Dragon as he was nicknamed, had his bachelor town-house. He was the ugliest man in Glasgow. Tall and gaunt he had an inward bend to his back and an enormous head with one blind eye, one squint eye and a Roman nose that twisted to one side until it nearly lay flat on his cheek. Bob Dragon had an appreciation of beauty and used to follow admiringly any pretty girl he saw in Argyle Street, only being diverted if he noticed another prettier girl coming the opposite way. Then he would about turn and follow her until an even more beautiful one caught his eye and changed his direction and so on, backwards and forwards, criss-cross, round and round.

If Bob Dragon had still been alive he would certainly have followed Julie as she crossed the Victoria Bridge swinging her handbag, admiring the view of the river and the other bridges curving across it. Bouncily she sang to herself a tune that was always being played on the wireless:

"Praise the Lord, and pass the ammunition.
Praise the Lord, and pass the ammunition . . ."

Now at the other side, her feet were on Gorbals ground. The Victoria Bridge led straight into Gorbals Street, the Main Street, and five minutes along it brought her to Gorbals Cross.

Her heart warmed to the old grey tenements. Their age, their cosy familiarity made her feel wonderfully safe. They crowded round her winking their tiny glass eyes in the sun, their close mouths dark caves of shelter.

Children in multi-coloured clothes swirled and bobbed around all the streets like vegetables in a broth pot.

Street songs and games frothed into the air.

"The big ship sails through the eeley ally o'
    The eeley ally o'
    The eeley ally o'
    The big ship sails through the eeley ally o' . . ."

Little girls were playing peaver and Julie hopped into their midst and took a kick at the peaver.

"Hey you!" somebody shrilled. "Whit do you think yer daein'?"

Further along others were intent on another game.

"In and out the dusty blue-bells,
    In and out the dusty blue-bells . . ."

Reaching the Cross, Julie waved to her father who was at the corner rubbing his hands and shuffling from one foot to the other, and showing all his gums like a delighted infant as he laughed with a neighbour. Immediately he spied her, he returned her wave and scuttled up their close to go and put on the kettle.

Gorbals Cross was really a circle with an iron-railinged Gents' underground lavatory and a clock standard in the middle. Four streets led off the centre like spokes of a wheel. Their close was on the corner of Gorbals Street and she crossed the road towards it and entered its dark tunnel-way swinging her handbag and jauntily whistling.

As usual Julie went in to attend to Mrs Goldberg before going upstairs to her own house and by that time her father had the tea-pot ready on the table and was taking the fish suppers from the oven where they had been keeping warm since he brought them from the local fish-and-chip shop.

Before starting to eat she filled a big kettle and also a pot full of water and put one on the gas ring and the other on the fire to heat. As well as hot water to wash the greasy dishes after the meal, she needed water to wash her hair and also her underwear and the blouse she planned to wear to Kelvinside the next day.

Immediately the meal was over she chased her father out of the way with a few extra shillings in his pocket and reckless orders to enjoy himself.

"Be like me, Dad, get happy!"

She decided to leave the dishes and see to her hair and the washing first. Then while her hair and the washing were drying she could clear the table. Tomorrow morning would be time enough to tidy the room.

On Saturdays, with helping Mrs Goldberg, she never had time to do anything in her own place and although her dad always bought the Saturday fish suppers, infused the tea and emptied the suppers from their newspaper wrappings on to the plates, that, and seeing that the fire did not go out during the day, was his sole contribution to the domestic scene.

The newspaper wrappings were still crushed in a heap on the table where he had discarded them and as usual he had put the milk bottle out instead of using a jug and the sugar bag instead of emptying the sugar into a bowl and he had cut the bread in thick ragged hunks.

As she rolled her hair up in curlers she sighed at the mess. He was an awful man. He had not even emptied the ashpan and it overflowed on to the tin sheet with the painted artificial tiles on the floor in front of the fire until the ashes reached the fender. Not that she blamed him. There was something terribly humiliating in the predicament of a man who had done a man's job for so many years, having to stay at home and do women's work while the woman of the house went out to earn the money.

It was pathetic how pleased he was when he won a few shillings on a horse. No matter how much she protested, he insisted on going halfers with her.

"Here you are, hen!" He would present the money with a nonchalant flourish. "You deserve it. Go and treat yersel tae something. Have a treat on your auld dad."

He and Reggie had got on like a house on fire. Her father had been such an eager enthusiastic listener that Reggie had become quite flattered and carried away with himself. He had recounted all his exploits in the air with gesticulations and noisy sound effects like a little boy swooping about the room with a toy aeroplane.

"By God!" Her father could not contain his delight and admiration. "You're a rerr lad, Reggie. Ah'll be damnt proud tae huv you fur a son!"

She was determined that she would be as big a hit with Reggie's folk. Why not, after all? She knew how to behave and how to dress. She had good taste. She was neither ignorant nor common. To talk with a posh accent was easy too. She talked posh in the shop every day. She would not overdo anything, of course. A lady never went to extremes.

Tomorrow when she went to Kelvinside she would be well groomed but discreet in her black suit, and white gloves and blouse, and her mother's fine gold locket and her manners would be impeccable.

She lit a cigarette, lay back on the chair by the fire and put her feet up on the side of the old black range.

Through the cloud of tobacco smoke she dreamed her dreams.

She heard the knock on the door and automatically bawled, "Come on in, it's no' locked."

Her mind was still in Kelvinside watching herself being a hit with Reggie's mother. Then, suddenly, Reggie's mother was standing in front of her.

There could be no mistaking the dainty woman in the pink suit that made her own best black costume look like something out of Woolworth's.

Julie stared at the confection of pink hat and the exquisite pink and white face underneath it. She was too stunned to drop her feet down or stub out her cigarette.

At last she forced herself to rise. Apologies lumped in her throat. Apologies for her sweaty feet, swollen with standing in the shop all day, apologies for her head, an ugly mass of steel curlers, apologies for the bottle of beer that she had been using for a hair rinse, apologies for the shameful state of the house. She swallowed down the lump and it left a bitter taste.

Her stare hardened, became impudent. She plumped her hands on her hips and arched her brows.

"Well?"

The other woman glanced around with only a suspicion of distaste before enquiring in reasonable moderate, ladylike tones.

"May I sit down?"

# Chapter Six

Muriel prayed for calmness as she lowered herself gracefully into a chair and eased off her gloves. Never in her whole life had she been in such a sordid place. Never in her worst nightmares had she imagined such a monstrous partner for Reggie. The girl was as common as dirt. There was a brazen impudent look about her. Hard emerald eyes glittered with venom and made Muriel feel afraid. With fast-fluttering heart she managed to speak:

"I take it you are Julie Gemmell."

"So?"

"I'm Mrs Vincent, Reggie's mother."

"Oh?"

"I thought we could have a little talk."

"Today."

"Yes."

"Not tomorrow."

"I thought it would be better to have a chat on our own."

"Why?"

Muriel longed for help and protection. Daggers of hurt tormented her. How could Reggie do this to her? she wondered.

"I'm worried about Reggie. He hasn't been himself recently. Oh, I know it's this awful war. It's upsetting everyone's lives. But I can't allow it to ruin Reggie's future as well as his present."

Julie lit a cigarette.

"I'm not with you, pal."

"What I'm trying to say is . . ." The older woman's

desperate gaze retreated for a moment. With trembling fingers she opened her handbag and plucked out a lace-edged hanky. "Poor Reggie is risking his life every day just now so that a decent future can be secured not only for himself but for everyone."

"So?"

"Reggie deserves a decent future."

"Sure!"

"But with the strain and pressures of the war, with everything mixed-up, people are making hasty and foolish decisions in their private lives, decisions they will later regret most bitterly."

Julie guffawed with laughter and flopped into a chair. Even the way she sprawled out had a defiant impudence.

"Look, Mrs Vincent, if you've come here to tell me I'm not good enough for you, why don't you just spit it out?"

"Not for me." Muriel's heart made a tight drum of her chest. "For Reggie."

"Reggie thinks I'm fine."

"At the moment he does."

"We're getting married on Monday. Haven't you heard?"

"That's why I'm here. I wouldn't have bothered if he had just had an affair and left it at that. It's perfectly understandable that men under such terrible tensions and dangers should want to indulge themselves when they can."

"You mean, sex?"

"But under normal circumstances they would never dream of marrying the person."

"You're a dirty-minded wee bitch."

Muriel felt ill. She prayed for Reggie or even Norman to come and carry her safely away from this claustrophobic, filthy beer-smelling slum. She longed to flee from the place. Only her love and concern for her son gave her enough courage to remain sitting.

"Reggie was going to marry a girl from Bearsden and

I was very happy for him. It's not that I object to Reggie getting married."

"So long as it's a girl from la-de-da Bearsden and not from common old Gorbals."

Julie's mimicry of her Kelvinside accent made Muriel flush.

"You are a most impertinent girl. I cannot imagine what my son sees in you."

"Too bad."

Muriel made to rise. Then forced herself down again. Her delicate pink face had gone an unhealthy white. She looked like a wax doll.

"I love Reggie. He's my only son. I cannot allow you to ruin his whole life."

"Look, pal, you can do what you like. You can talk yourself red, white and blue in the face. But nothing's going to change my mind about marrying Reggie on Monday."

"Why are you doing this to him? Is it for money? Is that it? I'll give you every penny I have if only you'll leave Reggie alone."

Julie sprang to her feet like a cat, green eyes sparking.

"How dare you come here and insult me! First of all you insinuate that I'm little better than a prostitute."

Clutching her handbag and gloves, Muriel rose too.

"You're putting words into my mouth."

"Then you try to buy me off with money."

"I'd sacrifice anything for my son's happiness."

"I don't want your lousy money. I don't want anything from you."

"What do you want?"

"Want! Want! That's the only way you can think. I know your type. I'm serving women like you every bloody day in Morton's. Spoiled, selfish little Modoms just like you! You don't care about Reggie or Reggie's happiness. All you're worried about is yourself. Your ideas, your wants, your plans."

"That's not true. You don't understand."

49

"I'm not daft. I understand all right. You've been spoiled rotten all your life. You've had it soft. You've had it all your own way. Well, not with me, pal. Not with me!"

Muriel closed her eyes and crushed her handkerchief against her mouth. At last she managed:

"Maybe I've said all the wrong things. If I have I'm sorry. I didn't mean to hurt you."

"You haven't hurt me, pal. You haven't bothered me one bit."

"Or insult you. I swear to you I'm not thinking about myself. The only one I care about is Reggie."

She held up a restraining hand to Julie who looked ready to flare into speech again.

"Oh, I admit I would have liked Reggie to marry Sandra Brodie and I had dreams of Reggie eventually having a partnership with Sandra's father. But I don't care about that any more. All I ask is that Reggie should not be rushed into a wartime marriage that he would later regret. That you might regret, too. My dear, I know it seems very exciting for things to happen suddenly. There's a certain glamour about all this impulsive, reckless behaviour, but what about afterwards? Do you really think you could fit in and be happy as a professional man's wife in middle-class suburbia?"

"I'm as good as you any day, anywhere, pal—and I'll make Reggie a good wife. One thing's obviously never occurred to you. *I* love him!"

"If you loved him you wouldn't marry him. You couldn't."

"That's the daftest thing I've ever heard."

"You know what I mean. You'll have to face up to the truth sometime. All I'm asking you, begging you, to do is face facts now before it's too late. You and Reggie have nothing in common, absolutely nothing. What basis is that for a marriage? You come from such different backgrounds and levels of education it just couldn't last. He'd end up hating you."

"You don't know what you're talking about."

"Oh, yes, my dear, I do—I know my son. He'd feel worried, then embarrassed, then trapped, then he'd hate you."

"He'll have no reason to feel any of these things. You're the only one who's likely to worry or embarrass Reggie. He's not going to thank you for coming over here badgering me for a start. Now do you want a cup of tea before you leave?"

"You know that I'm telling the truth."

"Mrs Vincent, Reggie and I are going to get on fine, just fine. Everything in the garden's going to be lovely, believe me."

"How can I believe you? Look at you! Look at this place!"

"I'm not in the habit of letting folk see me in my curlers." Julie's voice iced up with anger. "I never asked you to come here. And I haven't had all day to potter about the house like you. And I've been working hard in a shop from morning till night. Too bloody bad if I can't have a breather for five minutes after I come home without a la-de-da like you floating in and peering down your toffee-nose at me as if I were dirt. I'm as good as you, pal, and I've nothing to be ashamed of."

Just then the door opened to reveal a skeleton of a man with hollow toothless cheeks and shabby clothes that flapped loosely over his bones.

"Hey, whassup, eh? Is this toff upsettin' you, hen?" He staggered into the room belching beer and whisky fumes in Muriel's direction.

She looked away in disgust.

"I think I'd better leave."

"Hey, jussa minute, missus."

"Shut up, Dad."

Muriel heard the crack in the girl's voice and was moved to pity.

Going down the draughty stairs and out through the

dark tunnel to the street she felt harrowed by the whole encounter.

She had never before seen people living in such conditions. A whole new, distressing world opened up and she felt in danger of being swallowed by it.

She felt sick, claustrophobic, frightened. Her feet quickened towards home. If only she had never left Kelvinside. No good would come of her visit to the Gorbals. She knew that now.

What could she say to Reggie? That she had nothing against the girl personally? That she wasn't being snobbish or class-conscious?

But she *had* something against the girl. She was as common as dirt. She was ignorant and impudent. She belonged to filthy, sordid surroundings and had a dreadful unemployed drunk for a father. How *could* such a person be suitable for Reggie? The very idea was preposterous.

Reggie might think she was interfering or causing trouble for him just now, but later he would understand and he would thank her.

She would do everything in her power to dissuade him from making a fool of himself. She would plead, weep, have hysterics if necessary. She would become ill. She would tell him that she would die rather than see him go through with this ridiculous farce of a wedding.

Yet all the time she knew the worst was going to happen. She thought of the little boy who had trotted beside her on his way to school and all the hopes she had always cherished for him.

Bewildered and completely broken-hearted she kept asking herself, "Reggie, how could you?"

# Chapter Seven

The taxi crawled across the River Clyde like a black beetle through a yellow flame. Then suddenly darkness sucked it under the Stockwell Street railway bridge. A fusty smell filled the cab and people's feet echoed.

Julie shivered.

"Are you all right?" Catriona asked.

"Of course! Why shouldn't I be?"

Sunshine again as they curved into Argyle Street, then up Hope Street to West George Street.

"Maybe they'll be there after all."

"His people? Not a chance. Not after Saturday."

"Fancy her turning up like that. What rotten bad luck."

Julie whirled round, her face softly shaded by her wide brimmed hat, her green eyes luminous.

"She did it on purpose! That woman meant to humiliate me. I'll never forgive her. I'll never forgive that woman as long as I live."

Catriona mentally wrung her hands.

"Maybe she just thought . . ."

"She thought she could stop me marrying Reggie, but she's had to think again, hasn't she!"

"It's a pity, though. I mean, with you not having a mother of your own . . ."

"I'm a big girl now. I don't need the likes of her." Julie rustled the skirt of her taffeta dress and tugged at its matching bolero jacket. "Are you sure I'm all right?"

"You look lovely."

"Well, don't say it as if I'm about to be executed. Let's

53

get one thing straight before we get out of this car. I don't want you letting me down by howling and blubbering."

Catriona's head nodded in silent abject agreement.

"Come on, then!" Rustling and flouncing and keeping a good grip of her hat, Julie alighted from the taxi.

A noisy navy-blue and white wedding group of WRNS and matelots were being bullied into position for a photograph on the pavement. Another party spilled from the building, the bride and bridesmaid in square-shouldered utility costumes on which the roses on their lapels looked as incongruous as the pink carnations pinned to the coarse khaki uniforms of their partners.

Reggie and another young man in air-force blue were waiting inside. At the sight of Reggie, Julie flushed and her chin tilted in the air, but her attempt at nonchalance failed and she looked more in love and vulnerable than ever. Reggie linked arms with her and their eyes exchanged caresses as if they had already made some sort of holy communion.

Catriona felt so distressed, so desperate for escape, it was as much as she could do not to turn tail and run.

"You look wizard, Julie," Reggie said. "Doesn't she, Jeff? Didn't I tell you?"

Jeff's moustache vied in luxuriance with Reggie's handle-bar of blond hair, and his hearty guffaw made Catriona cringe.

Yet another bride and groom and bridesmaid and best man exploded past them as they tried to squeeze into the room in which the marriage ceremony was to take place.

It was bare, like a waiting-room only smaller, containing just a desk at which sat a dull-eyed, middle-aged man. He stared pityingly at Julie and Reggie. Then he rose with a sigh.

"Will all of you please stand in front of the desk. Has the best man got the ring?"

The ceremony consisted of identification, a brief explanation and finally an oral declaration by both parties.

Reggie spoke in a clear polite voice.

"I know of no legal impediment to my marrying this woman, Julie Gemmell, and I now accept her as my lawful wedded wife."

Gazing up at him, Julie repeated:

"I know of no legal impediment to my marrying this man, Reginald Vincent, and I now accept him as my lawful wedded husband."

Catriona began to weep.

They were back out in the corridor in less than ten minutes.

That's all it takes to ruin your life, Catriona thought. In a few minutes, a mere snowflake of time, you can step over, change paths, start on a narrow road of suffering too private, too complex, too terrible for a free person to understand.

The years of her marriage to Melvin weighed down, pressed in, choked her like the MacNair building on the night of the air-raid.

"For pity's sake, Catriona!" Julie laughed. "This is the happiest day of my life, and look at you! I've heard about people crying at weddings but this is ridiculous!"

Water gushed down Catriona's cheeks and she stuffed a handkerchief tightly against her mouth. It was a still silent kind of weeping. She just stood there, eyes open wide and tears overflowing.

They were all laughing. People laughed as they surged past defying the rule not to litter the place with confetti. The air shimmered with colour.

Wiping her face, Catriona began to laugh, too.

She allowed herself to be thrust outside to the waiting cab. Soon they were honking towards The Rogano licensed restaurant and from there to Green's Playhouse to dance to Joe Loss and his band. The dance-hall was on the top floor. Underneath it, Green's Playhouse Cinema boasted the biggest seating accommodation in Europe.

The lift spilled them out and Julie grabbed Catriona's hand and almost skipped into the ladies' cloakroom.

"Gosh, that wine's gone to my head!" She rolled her eyes and pretended to stagger. "Casheeona, aye shink aym a lirrle tiddly!"

"Stop it!" Catriona hissed with embarrassment and nudged her and darted a look around. Then feeling reassured that no one was paying them any attention, she captured an explosion of giggles in her hands. "I feel quite light-headed myself!"

Julie clenched her fists, screwed up her face and closed her eyes.

"I'm so happy, happy, happy, and I want you to be happy too."

Catriona had an affectionate impulse to hug her friend, but instead she laughed and said:

"Tonight I'll forget all my troubles and really enjoy myself, just to please you!"

They squeezed their way through the crowd of girls in front on the wall mirror and pushed their faces close to the glass to concentrate on smearing lips, and curling eyelashes and tidying eyebrows with stiff wet pinkies.

A high-pitched crescendo of chatter beat against the walls and filled the cloakroom with heady excitement. Outside men laughed and smoked and mooched and chewed gum while Joe Loss pounded the building with the bouncy "In The Mood".

After fluffing powder over their faces and lightly teasing their curls, and screwing round to check the backs of their dresses and the seams of their stockings, Julie and Catriona pushed through the swing doors and rejoined Reggie and Jeff.

The foyer was just a raised part at the back of the hall and in a couple of minutes they had descended the steps into the ballroom. It was a huge hall with pillars holding up a balcony where people sat at small tables littered with ash and empty cigarette and chewing gum packets and sipped lemonade and coffee. At one end of the floor, raised on a stage, Joe Loss in white tie and tails jumped and twisted and flashed his teeth and flayed the air with his baton. His men earnestly pulsated and blared out and pulsated and blared out above the bobbing heads of the dancers.

Julie and Reggie melted into one another's arms and floated away, cheek to cheek. Jeff gripped Catriona tightly against him and swooped her off with long fast strides that kept speeding unexpectedly into dainty spring-toed steps. She was never quite quick enough for this change of pace and kept stumbling and tramping on his feet.

Other dancers jostled them as people vigorously contorted themselves about. Men threw women high in the air and twisted them round their bodies like snakes and swooped them down to slide between their legs. Women bounced and twitched and twirled, skirts spun and opened like umbrellas to show wide-legged French knickers. Plum lips and rosy cheeks glistened and thin pencilled brows arched high with effort and excitement.

Catriona giggled. "I'm trampling all over you. I'm sorry. I'm afraid I'm not used to drinking so much wine. I feel quite dizzy." She pushed without success at his shoulders to try to lever him off.

The drink, the music, the heat, the frenzied people all intensified her reckless need to be happy, but to be happy she needed to escape from Jeff. The mere fact that he had a moustache was enough to remind her of Melvin.

"Please, Jeff, let me go. I want to stand at the side for a breath of air from the window."

Her voice wheedled and softened with promise and Jeff gave one of his excited whinnies and led her from the floor. Once out of his grip she felt delirious with freedom, pleaded with him to go and fetch her a glass of lemonade, then as soon as his back was turned she slipped away to hide by herself.

She could have swirled around and danced by herself and shouted to everyone that tonight she did not care about anything. Instead she edged through the crowds whispering,

"Excuse me, please, excuse me," and avoided people's eyes and kept her gaze lowered shyly.

She had never been to a dance before. She had barely finished school when Melvin wrenched her from her mother's apron strings and installed her in his house in Dessie Street. Now, for the first time, she caught a glimpse of a dimension to life she had been missing. Not that she wanted to participate; she felt much safer being a spectator, an observer of the scene. It was more than enough to listen to the music, to watch the dancers, to quickly brush against the men as she passed, and feel the heat of them and smell the tobacco and the sweat, and the cloying perfume of the women.

But a hand gripped her elbow and stopped her in her tracks like a startled doe and before she knew what was happening she was in a sailor's arms and shuffling with him cheek to cheek.

Up on the platform someone mouthed close to the microphone:

> "All of me . . .
> Why not take
> All of me . . . ?"

The lights had gone out and a spinning ball of mirrors sprinkled a confetti of colour through the darkness.

The sailor did not speak but held her with comfortable familiarity and after the dance he kept a grip of her hand and smiled and winked at her before drawing her to him for the next dance.

She noticed the Canada flash on his shoulder and wondered what Canada could be like. Before the war she had only heard Canada and America mentioned at school. They were just statistics to be learnt parrot-fashion for exams. They never had seemed real places where real people lived, reality had always been bounded by Glasgow.

"What's Canada like?" she asked curiously.

His voice in reply was a slow, gentle drawl that enchanted her.

"It's God's own country, honey! God's own country!"

"What a wonderful voice!"

He eased her back for a moment to give her a lopsided grin and an amused stare.

"I guess you're the sweetest little thing this side of the pond!" he drawled.

Wide-eyed against his chest she watched the speckled dancers drift around. It seemed as if she were in fairy-land.

The sailor was called Johnny and was French Canadian, she discovered later over a glass of lemonade. He talked nostalgically of a lovely old city called Montreal, Quebec, and how his father had been a peace-time skipper on one of the boats that worked the great lakes.

Catriona listened entranced, elbows propped on the small table, hands clasped under chin, as she gazed admiringly at the sapphire blue eyes, the tanned face crinkling kindly.

They danced again and again. The bank played the haunting "Lili Marlene" and everybody sang.

They were still clinging together and moving round the floor in a kind of dream when the band played the last dance.

"You must remember this . . .
A kiss is just a kiss . . .
A sigh is just a sigh . . ."

"You're wearing a wedding ring, honey," he murmured. "Does that mean there's a husband somewhere you're crazy about?"

Suddenly the impact of her personal tragedy drained her happiness away. She had not only lost a child, she had lost her own life too. In the middle of a song called "As Time Goes By" she remembered about Melvin.

"I'm afraid I'll have to go now," she told the sailor abruptly.

"Can't I see you home?"

"No, I'm sorry."

In a panic of distress she fled before he could speak to her again. A whirlpool of dancers sucked her away and by the time she reached the other side of the hall she had lost sight of him. She caught a glimpse of Jeff laughing and talking and obviously making a hit with a warm-eyed brunette. Julie and Reggie were nowhere to be seen.

The colourful, crowded scene disturbed her all the way back to Farmbank. The feel of it, the sight of it, the sound of it, each facet of the experience stayed alive and became more vivid in contrast to the house in Fyffe Road.

Everyone was in bed and, after checking that the boys were safely asleep, Catriona retreated to the living room and to her horse-hair sofa prison where she crouched in an almost unendurable fever of restlessness.

# Chapter Eight

"I won't let you down, Reggie. You'll never need feel ashamed because I come from a working-class family."

"Of course not, darling." He folded his uniform neatly over a chair beside the bed. "You talk such rot at times. Who worries about class nowadays?"

"Your mother!"

"Oh, I know how you must feel about Mother, but, honestly, she isn't as bad as you think. I admit she's old-fashioned, a minister's daughter and all that, but give her time. You'll find her pretty decent once you get to know her."

"Do you think I ever will?"

"For my sake you will."

"Oh? You're very sure of yourself."

"I'm sure of you."

"That doesn't sound very complimentary."

"You do love me, don't you, Julie?"

His eyes became suddenly very young and anxious. In a face that confidently sported a handlebar moustache and sideboards his youthful uncertainty seemed incongruous but it was an incongruity matched by the vest and pants and woollen socks he was wearing.

Julie giggled.

"I'm glad you don't wear Long Johns!"

She lay in bed happily watching him. She did not care in the slightest if he looked ridiculous. For better or for worse, he was her man, and a background of the crowded tenements had long ago taught her the true facts of life.

She had romance, she was bubbling over with the excitement of her whirlwind romance with an RAF officer, but she had no romantic illusions. Reggie was her man and that was that. In the Gorbals no woman thought or spoke of her "husband", it was always her "man", and Julie felt there was something basic, fundamental and right about the expression. It got back to the root of things, to the time of the cavemen when a woman depended on a man's physical strength to protect her or to kill something so that they could eat and survive. Yet woman's physical weakness had caused her to become much more wily and tougher in spirit, and there was something marvellously right about that too. One strength complimented the other. Sometimes the one strength helped to endure the other and that was as it should be.

She had watched marriage in close-up in the over-crowded tenements, seen husbands who worked hard and always handed over their wages and never raised their hand in anger. Their wives spoke proudly of "my man". She had seen other husbands who gambled and drank and beat their partners and their wives spoke of "my man" with the same possessive lilt to their voices.

Julie savoured the words as she watched Reggie strip off.

She had a wonderful feeling of completeness, of something accomplished that would never change. She did not like change. She had lived in the same house in the same district all her life. She had attended only one school. Her loyalties had clung tenaciously from childhood to a single friend until that friend married and moved to England. Since leaving school she had worked for only one firm.

Reggie was the first man she had ever loved and she was happy in the certainty that he would be the only love in her life.

She felt unashamedly proud of him. She felt like a cave-woman who not only fulfils the basic necessity of finding a mate but who succeeds in ensnaring the very best mate in the cave.

"I'll always love you," she told him.

He looked away, stubbed out his cigarette in the ashtray on the bedside locker.

"Damn this bloody war!"

As he said the words, Julie's quick eye saw his mind drift far away from her.

"Come to bed." She pushed the covers down to reveal white breasts bulging over a black nightdress. "Forget about the war."

He came in beside her and she sighed with satisfaction. "We're all that matter. We love each other and we belong to each other and we're here in this hotel in each other's arms. Nothing in the whole world could be more important."

She could feel him trembling against her and she was glad of her soft woman's skin and breasts and belly and full hips arching under his exploring hands. She was his and it was right and proper that he should be pleased with her.

Here was her strength and her love and generosity guided her in an infinite variety of ways to increase his pleasure until she was exhausted but triumphant and he was gasping for breath and half-weeping in her arms.

Gradually his jerky breathing soothed and after a long peaceful silence, she remarked:

"I think there's blood or something on the sheet."

"It's all right, darling," he murmured sleepily. "That happens when it's the first time."

"But it's on the sheet."

"Don't worry!"

"I can't stay the night in a hotel and leave dirty sheets on the bed next morning."

"Darling, the sheets are stripped off every morning."

"I'm not having people say that I left stained sheets."

"They'll know what it is. They probably gossip and laugh about these things all the time in hotels."

Immediately the bedclothes flurried back. She struggled up.

"Well, they won't get the chance to gossip or laugh about me!"

"What the devil are you doing?"

"Get up! Come on, I want that sheet! It won't take a minute."

"You're joking!"

She tugged the sheet from under him.

"It's only a small stain. I'll get rid of it in a couple of minutes at the washhand basin and then hang it over the chair at the window to dry."

"Good Lord!"

"I've got my pride, Reggie. I don't sleep in other folks' beds and leave stained sheets."

Her breasts jiggled about and she became pink in the face and breathless as she attacked the offending part of the sheet with a soapy nailbrush.

Reggie relaxed among the disorder of blankets with his arms folded behind his head and roared laughter up to the ceiling.

"Be quiet!" she scolded him. "Somebody might hear you. How would it look if we were chucked out the hotel for noisy behaviour in the middle of the night? I'd never live it down."

She held the crumpled linen under a gush of cold water and then wrung the water out, her face contorting with the exertion. "There, that's better. I told you, Reggie, I'll never let you down. I've got pride and I'm not afraid of hard work. I've always kept a spotless clean house and my mother before me."

Reggie grinned over at her. "You're only nineteen. What do you know about keeping house?"

"I've kept one for seven years. My mother died when I was twelve. Move over till I tidy the bed, you big oaf." Her voice softened reminiscently. "I remember Mammy, and my wee brother. He died just before her. There was first one funeral and then another, and do you know what sticks out most vividly in my mind?"

"What?"

"The worry about money—about not having any, I mean! Mammy used to worry about that all the time when she was alive. As long as we can manage to keep a roof over our heads and a brave face to the world—she always used to say. And she always managed. But at the funeral it was terrible. You know how there has to be a funeral tea for everybody. Well, talk about feeding the multitude with a loaf and a few fishes!"

She rolled her eyes. "I knew Mammy wouldn't have wanted me to borrow from anybody. But I thought it would be all right to take the stuff Mrs Goldberg offered. We always lit her fire and did odd jobs for her on Saturdays and I reckoned she owed us something." She cuddled into bed beside him. "Dad kept wailing—'I'm no use without my better half.' But I told him, 'We'll have to show everybody we can manage right from the start or they'll have me away in a home and you'll end up in "the Model" and what would Mammy think about the disgrace of that?'"

Reggie's arms tightened around her. "I want to look after you for the rest of your life. I don't want you to have to worry about money or anything ever again."

She sighed with happiness.

"Oh, Reggie, just think—we've our whole long lives before us. We've so much to plan and talk about. What kind of house do you reckon we'll have one day?"

"A small one, to start with anyway, modern and easy to run. Life's for living, old girl. I don't believe in women being chained to the kitchen sink and all that rot. No, we're going to enjoy life and we're going to live it together!"

"A bathroom's a must!"

"Definitely!"

"And a kitchenette. It's terrible this idea of sinks and cookers and beds all in the one room. I'd like to have met the man who designed Glasgow tenements. I'd have given him a piece of my mind."

"Tenements aren't all like that though, darling. You must see our flat. You'd love it."

"Your mother and father's, you mean?"

"Yes. I was hoping you could have stayed there while I was away."

"Reggie, your mother hates the sight of me! She made it perfectly plain she didn't even want to see me at her place on Sunday."

"She didn't mean it, darling. It was just the shock of everything. You must admit it was a bit sudden. In her day there were long courtships and everything was so different."

"Everybody knew their 'place', you mean? People from the Gorbals stayed in the Gorbals and never sullied the fair banks of the Kelvin?"

"Julie! She just didn't expect me to get married so suddenly, that's all!"

"That's what you think, pal! But anyway, what about my dad?"

"Oh, he has plenty of good friends and neighbours and plenty of time. He could manage. It's you I'm worried about. You work all day and then have to go back there. It's a bad show. I'd feel much better if you were in Botanic Crescent. Mother could have a good meal ready for you every night and you could relax and take things easy in civilised surroundings!"

She jerked up.

"There you are! You're as bad! I come from uncivilised surroundings, do I? Well, let me tell you I'm as civilised as your mother any day!"

"Darling!" He soothed and pulled her back down into his arms. "Idiot! I was talking about the lack of hot water in the houses, and cavity beds, and lavatories outside on the stairs and the cold draughty tunnels of closes. I know these things aren't your fault."

Her ruffled feathers gradually settled.

"Well . . . all right then."

"How about calling there tomorrow afternoon?"

66

She screwed up her face.

"Oh, Reggie . . ."

"I promise you, Mother won't slam the door on you if that's what you're worried about."

Julie sighed.

"You're fond of her, aren't you."

"She's my mother."

There was a little pause before she said, "I remember how I felt about Mammy right enough."

"Does that mean you'll come?"

"If it's what you want, Reggie."

"Oh, I love you, Julie!" His young voice trembled with gratitude and excitement. "And I know Mother will love you too. It's simply a matter of getting to know each other."

She suddenly became perky.

"I'll come on one condition. You come with me to the shop first."

"The shop?"

"Morton's, where I work. I want to show you off."

He laughed.

"Darling, you've got the day off. They'll think you're mad if you turn up."

"No, they won't. They'd love to meet you. Go on, Reggie, be a sport. There's just the manageress and the two alteration hands. You've met Catriona already."

"But why?"

"I told you. I'm proud of you and I want to show you off. I think you're the most handsome, the most wonderful, the cleverest man in the whole world!"

"Hold on, old girl. Handsome, maybe, but clever never!"

"You fly these big 'planes. I've seen pictures of the instrument panels on some of them. I can't imagine how anybody could begin to understand them. You're an absolute genius as far as I'm concerned." She hugged him and showered him with kisses. "And I'll love you for ever and ever. Will we call into the shop tomorrow? Just for a couple of minutes on the way to your mother's."

67

"Righteo."

She immediately detected the note of false cheerfulness.

"What's wrong?"

"Oh, mentioning 'planes reminded me of the war and of having to go back to it tomorrow night."

"Reggie, I'm sorry. I shouldn't have said that."

"It's not your fault, darling."

"Can we come back here for a little while tomorrow night before you leave?"

"Yes, we'll just call on Mother for half an hour or so in the afternoon."

She snuggled closer to him and opened her mouth in eager invitation against his, and they made love again, and again, and again, until Reggie rolled over on to his back, his arms flopping helplessly at his sides.

Her mouth still slid over his body, warm and full and eager.

"Reggie," she urged.

"I don't think I could again, darling."

She kept forcing her face against him like a cat rubbing itself.

"Reggie," she whispered. "Reggie!"

# Chapter Nine

"Snap—snap—snap—snap! Grandpa, I said it first. I said it before you. I did! I did!"

Rab Munro roared with laughter as his broad baker's hands fought to snatch the cards from Fergus's eager grasp.

"No, you didn't. I won. Snap!"

"Grandpa! Give them to me! They're mine. I said it before you! Grandpa!"

Catriona could not stand it any longer. There was nothing wrong with a game of Snap but this one had been going on too long. It was nearly eleven o'clock and Fergus was getting far too excited. He would never be able to sleep.

"Daddy, that's enough. It's time Fergus was in bed."

"Och, Grandpa, don't listen to her. Come on!"

"Now, now!" Rab's lantern-jawed face lengthened into sternness. "None of your cheek, young Mr Skinamalink."

Fergus erupted into high-pitched giggles.

"You're an old Mr Skinamalink."

Catriona rose.

"Fergus, put the cards away now and no more nonsense. You've school in the morning."

"An old Skinamalinky long-legs with four eyes and frizzy hair."

Rab grimaced in mock rage and gave a giant-sized roar.

"What? Let me get my hands on that rascal. Fee-fi-fo-fum! I smell the blood of an Englishman!"

Fergus began to squeal with excitement and brought Andrew skipping into the room in striped pyjamas. His grandmother had been bathing him and his curly hair was matted and showed patches of white scalp. Freckles peppered the bridge of his nose and his cheeks were scarlet beacons. Gleefully he joined in the shouting.

"Fee—fo—fi—fum!"

"Now don't you start. This is ridiculous, Mummy. He should have been in bed hours ago. I'm getting worried about their health."

"Oh, be quiet!" Hannah Munro pushed her daughter aside in disgust. "You're a bit late with your worrying. If you had worried when you'd reason to worry, my wee Robert would have been alive today. That lovely wee pet who did nothing but smile at everyone."

Rab tugged off his reading glasses and tossed them aside.

"Now can you see what I've had to suffer all these years, Catriona? She never gives up. She goes on and on."

"Oh, yes, you'd like me to keep quiet, wouldn't you? It would be much easier for you if you were just allowed to drink all your wages away every week and play around with any woman you fancied."

"Too bad if a man can't have an odd pint of beer to wash the flour dust away."

"Grandpa, play with me!" Fergus yelled. "Play with me! Play with me!"

Catriona determinedly began scooping up the cards.

"Fergus, you're giving me a headache. It's eleven o'clock at night and time you boys were in bed. Now off you go. I won't tell you again."

Andrew glowered and for the first time Catriona saw a look of Melvin about him.

"Granny said I could stay up until I got a cup of cocoa and a piece on jam."

Hannah patted his head.

"That's right, Andy. You tell her."

Rab groaned.

"There's no need to encourage the child to be cheeky.

70

She is his mother, you know. Or have you conveniently forgotten that important fact?"

"There's a few things you've conveniently forgotten, Robert."

"Oh, no, no, you'd never allow me to do that." His big-boned frame sunk back into his clothes and he added bitterly more to himself than to her: "On my deathbed you'll be standing over me casting up every fault I've ever had."

"Grandpa! Grandpa! I've got the cards!"

"Fergus, give those to me at once!" Catriona's voice sharpened with irritation.

She had been on her feet all day at the shop and since she had arrived home there had not been one minute's peace and quiet.

"There you are!" With gales of laughter Fergus tossed the pack of cards high in the air scattering them around every corner of the room. Almost at the same time Catriona's hand shot out and smacked him across the face.

His laughter collapsed into an offended whine then jerked into broken-hearted sobbing.

Immediately Andrew burst into tears of sympathy and apprehension.

Catriona put her hands to her ears.

"Oh, shut up! Shut up! Get to bed, both of you!"

Miserably they trailed off, wiping their wet cheeks with their sleeves.

Hannah at last found her voice.

"That's terrible! I'll talk to you in a minute, my girl. Come on, boys, Granny'll give you a nice cup of cocoa and a piece'n'jam in bed."

After they'd left the room Catriona said to her father:

"Jam in bed! They'll get into a sticky mess and their teeth will be ruined."

"You shouldn't have hit the boy."

"I didn't mean to. It happened before I could stop

71

myself." Abruptly she changed the subject. "Daddy, I've been looking for a place of my own."

His dark eyes filled with alarm and she got a glimpse of how fond he really was of the children and how much their company meant to him. He did not say anything and she lowered her gaze to her hands and went on.

"I've got this room and kitchen in Byres Road—I just heard this morning. I didn't want to say anything until it was safely settled."

His balloon of tension puttered down with a sigh.

"Oh, well, it's your life, hen."

"You'll still be able to see the boys, Daddy. You know you'll be welcome to come over any time."

He nodded as if not trusting himself to speak. Then after a minute's silence he got up and at the living-room door he muttered without turning round:

"Time I was in bed, too."

Catriona ran towards him and hugged him before he left the room. If only her mother would take the news with equally quiet resignation.

The temptation to postpone telling Hannah was strong. Catriona would have liked to whisk the boys and old Duncan away to Byres Road and avoid the ordeal of breaking the news to her mother. But, for one thing, the old man was fuddled with drink most of the day and it was difficult enough to prise him out of the bedroom at meal-times. It was going to be a sizeable operation to transfer him from Farmbank to Byres Road. He would complain loudly and long about leaving his chair in front of the gas fire and having his radio-listening and his routine shuffle to the local off-licence interrupted.

The boys would not take kindly to leaving their grand-parents' house either, but desperation kept pushing Catriona on.

As soon as her mother came through, she burst out:

"Mummy, I've something to tell you."

"I've something to tell you, you wicked girl. Don't you

dare raise your hand to an innocent child. The Bible gives a warning about what can happen to anyone who does such a thing."

Her voice raised and filled out with the strong dignified tones she used when addressing the Band of Jesus. "'It would be better for him if a great millstone were hung round his neck and he were thrown into the sea. And if your hand causes you to sin, cut it off; it is better for you to enter life maimed than with two hands to go to hell, to the unquenchable fire.'"

"I've found another place to live. There isn't enough room for us here. It's not right that Da has your bedroom and . . ."

"Don't talk nonsense," her mother interrupted. "Mr MacNair is no bother at all. He's perfectly happy and comfortable in the bedroom."

"But you and Daddy . . ."

"Daddy and I are fine."

"The boys . . ."

"I know what's best for the boys. I'm older than you, Catriona. I've lived longer and learned more. I'll worry about the boys. Just you get to your bed. You're always complaining about being tired in the morning. Well, I'm not keeping you up." She made a grand sweeping gesture and it occurred to Catriona what a fine-looking woman she was with her thick burgundy-hair and strong tipped-up chin and rigid back. "There's the sofa and don't forget to say your prayers and remember to ask God's forgiveness for all your sins, especially for causing so much hurt to people."

"I mean it, Mummy. I'm grateful to you for having taken us all in after the air-raid. I don't know what we would have done without your help."

"That's something you've still to learn. Families are supposed to help one another. Now get to bed."

In a gesture of dismissal, Hannah began making preparation for the morning, striding backwards and forwards,

73

crashing dishes and cutlery about in the sideboard and clattering them on to the table.

"Mummy, I'm sorry, but whether you listen to me or not—whether you face it or not—I'm moving to Byres Road with Da and the children. It's all settled. I've paid the deposit and everything."

Her mother stopped.

"But you can't go."

"I must."

"You selfish, wicked girl. What about the children? What about their schooling? You're always whining on about that. This just shows the lies and the hypocrisy that's been coming out of your mouth. A lot you care about those poor boys."

"It's because I care . . ."

"May the good Lord forgive you, Catriona. You're talking about uprooting these children just when they've begun to get over the dreadful shock of what you done to them before."

Like a time bomb, Catriona exploded in hysteria.

"You keep blaming me for the air-raid! The quicker I'm out of here the better before you start blaming me for the whole bloody war!"

Hannah was shocked speechless for a minute. Her ruddy cheeks faded to reveal fragile threads of purple capillaries criss-crossing. But she remained bolt upright. She lost none of her dignity.

"How dare you!" The words were savoured slowly and with a very correct accent. "How dare you use bad language to your own mother. Little did I think I'd ever live to see the day my own daughter would sink so low. Get to your bed at once. I don't want to hear another word from you. You're not fit to be in charge of young children."

Catriona wept with frustration and distress.

"It's all settled," she repeated helplessly.

"Well, you can just unsettle it!"

"I can't stay here forever. There's Melvin."

"What about Melvin?"

"There isn't enough room for us. What happens when Melvin comes home? Where could he sleep?"

"There's no question of that man coming back here for years and years yet."

"No, you're wrong! The war could finish quite soon. They say there's going to be a big invasion any day now. The Allies are ready to pour across the Channel and sweep the Germans off the map."

"Who says?"

"Everyone says."

"Everyone's been saying things like that for the past two years."

"Maybe they don't know when or where or how, but something's bound to happen soon. We keep getting customers in the shop who've travelled around, especially down south, or have had word from there because you can't get into some of the places now—they're so packed with soldiers and sailors and equipment."

"Glasgow's been packed for years."

"Yes, but nothing like what they say. They say every inch of sea for miles around Britain and every river and every port is chock-a-block with warships and all sorts of queer landing-craft and artificial harbours and things. And there's so many more ships being built they're even putting them together in streets and children can stand on their own doorsteps and watch the welders and riveters."

"What nonsense!" Hannah scoffed. "And don't try and evade the issue, my girl. These children through in that room are perfectly happy and content where they are and you have absolutely no excuse for uprooting and upsetting them just now."

"It isn't nonsense, Mummy. The streets are full of army trucks and tanks and guns as well, lines and lines of them, half up on pavements in front of houses and folks having to squeeze past or walk out on the road to get round them.

"Well, if it's God's plan to have an invasion—there will be an invasion. So stop whining on about it and get to your bed."

"I was just explaining how Melvin might get home sooner than we expect and I've got to be ready. I've got to have a place for him to come to."

"You don't care about that man. Why you married that man I'll never know."

"So that's why I've got this wee room and kitchen in Byres Road."

"You've not even any idea bout how to manage with rations. You were lucky before. You got extras from the old man's shop. Now the only way to manage is to pool all our books and coupons the way we've been doing. And I'm well known and respected at the shops along the road and if there's anything special comes in they let me know or keep a share aside for me. You don't know a soul in Byres Road. Now I'm tired, if you're not, and I'm going to my bed. I don't want to hear another word from you. I've had enough of your stupid selfish talk for one night."

"But, Mummy . . ." Catriona began again then stopped in mid-air.

There was no use talking.

# Chapter Ten

Restrained by roll upon roll of barbed wire, Britain was shrinking fast. Overcrowding had become claustrophobic. There was no longer any escape from the uniformed multitude jostling shoulder to shoulder with the civilian population.

Noisy activity whirled to a climax. Ports seethed with an astonishing variety of shipping. More and more vessels kept crowding in. Ships sprang up everywhere, not only in shipyards. In narrow streets and alleyways, in workshops round every corner, steel skeletons clanged and reverberated.

Into the small island crushed more and more assembly points, ammunition dumps, vehicle parks, camps, training-grounds, embarkation "hards", barbed wire, airfields, anti-aircraft and searchlight sights. Day and night fast convoys roared at breakneck speeds in endless streams along narrow streets making houses shudder and echo to the thundering of wheels.

On 6th April 1944 all military leave was stopped. Troops and armoured vehicles crammed the coast ten miles deep. Plans for each day and enormous feeding and other necessary arrangements had to be made. In trucks lining seaside streets, typewriters clicked busily. Orders were triplicated in mobile offices complete down to wastepaper baskets.

A vast armada of ships swelled the waters of every port and harbour and buffeted for space with thousands of "things" that floated like the huge artificial harbours called Mulberries.

Restless confined men played cards and thought of women and beer and home and argued about invasion dates.

In great concentrations of armoured equipment the sound of bagpipes could be heard as Highland units, destined to be the spearhead in France, practised for the final piping of troops into battle.

On 2nd June the ships had begun loading and by the early hours of 5th June every craft was crammed and some had already set off, the tin-hatted men down below jam-packed tightly, lumpy with equipment and guns clashing against each other. By four a.m. the recall went out by broadcasts from the shore for their return because the weather had worsened. Fog closed in but the civilian population could hear the continuous thunder high above them in the darkness as thousands of RAF and American Air Force night bombers set out to bombard the coastal batteries commanding the landing beaches to be assaulted.

In the landing craft the packed troops tried to get some sleep while a ferocious gale made the vessels roll and heave and plunge and smack waves against thin plates. Men vomited and had to remain in their vomit, and the stench mixed with silent fear and tobacco and khaki sweat.

On 6th June, General Eisenhower's order of the day was read by commanders to all troops:

"Soldiers, sailors and airmen of the Allied Expeditionary Force, you are about to embark on the great crusade towards which we have striven these many months. The eyes of the world are upon you. The hopes and prayers of liberty-loving people everywhere march with you.

"In company with our brave allies and brothers-in-arms on other fronts you will bring about the destruction of the German war machine, the elimination of Nazi tyranny over the oppressed peoples of Europe and security for ourselves in a free world.

"Your task will not be an easy one. Your enemy is well trained, well equipped and battle-hardened. He will fight savagely but this is the year 1944. Much has happened since the Nazi triumph of 1940–1. The United Nations have inflicted upon the Germans great defeats in open battle man to man. Our air offensive has seriously reduced their strength in the air and their capacity to wage war on the ground.

"Our home fronts have given us an overwhelming superiority in weapons and munitions of war and placed at our disposal great reserves of trained fighting men.

"The tide has turned. The free men of the world are marching together to victory.

"Good luck, and let us all beseech the blessing of Almighty God upon this great and noble undertaking."

In a creaky old destroyer in a channel choked with ships, Alec Jackson said:

"To hell with the whole thing! Just let me get back to Glasgow, mate!"

It was around seven in the morning and smudgy battle-ships and cruisers were steaming up and down drenching the shores of France with thunderous broadsides that killed French women and children as well as German men. Holiday houses and hotels gushed with fire.

Nearer the sea's edge spurts of flame shot up from the beaches in high snake-like ripples. Guns flashed and yellow cordite smoke curled into the air.

Invasion craft crawled down the ships' davits like beetles, and headed towards the shore in long untidy lines. Inside them the backs of men heaved as they vomited while bursts of spray broke over the sides and the craft smacked and lurched about. They tried to draw strength from the fact that everything had been meticulously planned; they had been trained for months for what was to come and there were officers to tell them where to go and what to do. They did not realise then how plans could go wrong, how orders could become impossible to fulfil and how quickly officers could get shot.

Sometimes when orders were given and blindly obeyed in true military fashion the men fared no better than in the American Sector of the beach code-named Omaha. There, tank-landing craft dropped their ramps in unexpectedly deep and stormy water and at exactly the correct time ordered, the first tank moved forward to drop like a stone and never be seen again. Commanders in the second, third and fourth tanks in each craft watched the first tanks and crews disappear and drown. They had orders to launch, however, and they launched. One by one they vanished beneath the waves without trace.

Within two or three minutes twenty-seven of the thirty-two tanks were at the bottom of the Channel and nearly one hundred and fifty men were drowned.

Only one commander away at the western end of the beach decided conditions were not favourable and waited until he could go right in and land his tanks on the shore.

In the crush of naval craft of all types incidents like those at Omaha went unnoticed.

Men were waiting silently in landing-craft, ears alert for the thudding of shells, hands clutching rifles. The wallowing of the craft eased as they approached shallower water and gently nosed through a mass of debris until an explosive jar lurched everyone forward.

Now they had arrived. Ex-office clerks and bricklayers, and shopkeepers and toolfitters and students were sharing the same apprehension. Now ramps crashed down, leaving them naked to machine-gun bullets that twisted them into grotesque ballet dancers and spattered the sea with scarlet. Now mothers' sons became butcher-meat caught up on barbed wire, became flotsam, became beach litter with faces buried in sand, became mere objects robbed of human dignity, rumps poking in the air.

Wave upon wave of men were spewed out to trample over the dead and dying to get a foothold in France.

Beyond the beaches glider-planes crashed and glider-planes landed and paratroopers speckled the earth with white and desperately shouted the rallying cries they had been taught.

"Able—Able!"

"Baker—Baker!"

"Charlie—Charlie!"

They were not surprised at being lost or confused. They had been told before setting out:

"Do not be daunted if chaos reigns. It undoubtedly will."

On HMS *Donaldson* Alec felt he had been plunged into the centre of a maelstrom of hell. Noise was incredible and continuous. German shore batteries duelled with the ships. The whole shoreline flashed with white from the big guns, plumes of smoke curled high in the air and blood-red flames rampaged out then shrank under billowing clouds of dirty smoke.

Above, a constant umbrella of bombers and fighters darkened the sky. The air groaned and throbbed with the engines of the heavy bombers, and fighters streaked noisily underneath them.

Alec shaded his eyes with his hands and peered back towards home. He had never seen so many aircraft in his life. He wondered where they were all coming from. Britain was a small island and there were limits to what it could hold. Surely there could never have been enough ground space for all these 'planes to take off. Yet they kept being tossed skywards. They were still zooming over.

His tired eyes, gritty and bloodshot, trailed after one massive formation as it roared above him and away across France. He saw some of the 'planes explode in the high distance like red cherries and others dive down, charcoaling the sky with black lines.

"Poor bastards!" he muttered.

Never before in his life had he felt so disgusted, so sick to his guts.

"What am I doing here?" he asked himself.

Suddenly the whole thing seemed like a horrible charade.

The padre had led them in prayer before it began and asked for God's blessing. The German padres would no doubt have asked the same God the same thing. It was ludicrous.

He remembered Madge telling him about some Quaker set Catriona had got to know. Apparently that lot believed there was a bit of God in every man. He remembered how Madge had joked about it.

"A bit of the devil in you, more like!"

Now his normally good-natured mind twisted with sarcasm.

"Well, if there's a bit of God in every man, mate, this day man's being bloody disrespectful to his Maker."

Thinking of Madge brought memories of his children crowding in.

Since he had been in the Navy they had grown away from him. They were like strangers. More and more his thoughts turned to them as they had been before when they were all at home and carefree and happy together. As ships turned broadside on and belched destruction towards the shore he saw his children through the sheet of flame. They had polished faces, white bibs, and sat at the kitchen table. They were singing and banging time with their spoons.

Above the bedlam of war he heard their reedy voices:

> "It's a long way to Tipperary,
> It's a long way to go.
> It's a long way to Tipperary,
> To the sweetest girl I know.
> Goodbye Piccadilly,
> Farewell Leicester Square—
> It's a long, long way to Tipperary,
> But my heart's right there."

# Chapter Eleven

"How can I ever repay you, Julie?" Catriona longed to cling to her friend and weep tears of thankfulness on her shoulder but she kept emotion in check.

She was always uncertain of Julie's reactions. Julie had a perky brusqueness that seemed to repel displays of affection as if they were a weakness or an embarrassment she had no patience for. Yet at times she gave the impression of being a bouncing time bomb of emotion herself.

No use embracing or kissing Madge in an attempt to show gratitude either. She had already tried that and Madge had knocked her roughly aside with one of her big hearty laughs.

"For God's sake, hen, grow up. Stop acting so stupid!"

Julie shrugged and lit a cigarette. "What have I done except give you a few old cups and plates and a couple of chairs?"

"And all the other things. Both of you have been absolutely marvellous. Gosh, I can hardly believe it. A place of my very own." She closed her eyes with the relief of it. "I can do what I like, come and go as I like, please myself about everything."

"What an imagination!" Madge laughed. "You're a scream, hen. You've spent all your savings on the deposit for a wee room and kitchen that's really your man's and you're having to share it with two weans and an old man. Still, you're lucky to get any place. Houses aren't so easy to come by nowadays. And you're not so crowded as me, eh?"

"Yes, no harm to your new house, Catriona." Julie strolled over to the window puffing smoke as she went. "But better you than me living here."

Catriona's small face tightened with anxiety.

"Why? What's wrong with the place? Byres Road's supposed to be a good district, isn't it? I know this isn't the best building in the road, but there's a lovely view. You can see the Botanic Gardens."

"It's too near my mother-in-law, that's why." Julie's green eyes suddenly twinkled with mischief. "Just think, she'll probably pass here every day going for her messages. Maybe one day a bus'll get her crossing Great Western Road."

"Julie! Don't tempt Providence by saying things like that!"

Madge tucked a straggle of hair behind one ear, shifted her pregnant belly to a more comfortable position and gave a toothy grin.

"Is she an old cow, hen?"

"Tairaibly Kailvainsaide, yew know!" Julie rolled her eyes. "Tairaibly refained and all that. She nearly died when she found out about me. She thinks I'm dirt because I come from the Gorbals. I told her straight. I'm as good as you and better, pal. Reggie told her as well. You ought to have heard him. Reggie's loyal and all that. He's fond of his mother but, as he says, now that we're married his wife comes first. He'd do anything for me." She gave a long sigh. "He's so handsome too. Isn't he, Catriona?"

"Tall and broad-shouldered with marvellous blue eyes and blond hair," Catriona enthused, happy to have found a way to be of service to Julie.

Madge stretched her big frame out on one of the chairs.

"Aye, they're all great lads at first. I remember when I used to think my man was marvellous."

Julie coloured with the sudden intensity of her feelings.

"But Reggie *is* marvellous! He really is! He's the nicest, most wonderful person I've ever met. He's such a

84

gentleman and so well educated. He's been to the university, hasn't he, Catriona? Yet there's no side about him at all. My dad and him got on like a house on fire. One time he took my dad out and bought him a drink. I'm not kidding you, everybody in the Gorbals met Reggie that day. Dad was so proud he was stopping strangers in the street and showing Reggie off."

Madge grinned and scratched the side of her breast, making it swing and wobble about.

"Och, well, the best of luck to you, hen. You're only a wee lassie yet! I just hope you'll never be trauchled with a squad of weans in your wee place in the Gorbals the way I am in Springburn. I hope to God my crowd aren't ruining the Botanic Gardens across there just now. I'll murder them wee middens one of these days. They never pay a blind bit of notice to a thing I say."

"Oh, no!" Julie sent a confident stream of smoke darting from full pursed lips. "Reggie and I are only going to have two children, one of each sex. We've got everything planned."

Madge spluttered out a howl of derisive laughter. Catriona giggled before she could stop herself and immediately felt guilty and hastened to make amends.

"We know what you mean, Julie."

"Well, what are you laughing at? What's so funny?"

"We're a lot of bloody mugs, aren't we?" Madge remarked quite pleasantly. "We're that easy conned."

Julie's eyes lit with anger.

"What do you mean, conned? Nobody cons me."

"What Madge means is . . ." Catriona began, but Madge interrupted.

"Things don't turn out the way we bloody well plan, that's what I mean. If you don't keep your eye on that good-looking fella of yours, hen, the chances are some other lassie'll be having a squad of weans to him as well as you."

Julie's brows and her voice pushed high.

"My Reggie? You don't know him. He's so sincere and

sensitive. A perfect gentleman. Isn't he, Catriona?"

"Oh, gosh, yes!"

"I knew all I needed to know about my man the first time I looked at him."

"Well, hen, I'm sorry to be such a wet blanket but I still say you're just a wee lassie and you've a lot to learn. If you ask me, men are all the same—selfish, randy buggers. That's all they care about. All they want is to enjoy themselves. If you ask me, hen, you'll be trauchled with a dozen weans before you're done."

"I'm not asking you. I know my man!" The hand that stubbed at her cigarette trembled. "He's not selfish. But if he ever does decide that he wants more children, that's O.K. with me, pal. If my man wants a dozen kids, that's O.K. with me. Whatever my man wants is O.K. with me!"

Madge's freckled face spread into a smile and she hauled herself up.

"Well, the best of British luck to you, hen. I'd better go and round up my dirty wee middens while there's still some of the Botanic Gardens left. God, my varicose veins are killing me." She laughed. "I've piles now as well! They're some other things you're liable to get that you didn't plan for. Och, there I go again. It's a shame, isn't it! Don't pay any attention to me. The trouble with me is I've got such a rotten bugger for a man. Honest to God I hate that dirty midden."

An awkward silence followed as she struggled into the grey swagger coat she had made herself out of an old army blanket to save clothing coupons.

Catriona felt guilty and ashamed at the mere mention of Alec and she miserably lowered her head.

"And he'd better not say a word to me about his book money when he comes back or he'll get this down his throat." Madge brandished a red fist. "I had to keep dibbling into it to pay the doctor for the weans and all the things he said they were needing. That house of ours is that damp it gives them coughs and God knows all what, poor wee sods, and what with this new one . . . See, if Alec says anything about me not managing right with the money . . ."

"Madge, what are you getting all upset about?" Surprised Catriona looked up. "Alec's not the type to get on to you about money, is he? You've never said anything about him being like that before."

"Maybe it's my conscience bothering me." She sent a great gust of hilarity up to the ceiling. "I've spent all the bugger's money. Serves him bloody well right! Well, I'll away, Catriona. I'll see you next week, hen. Cheerio, Julie. Come over to Springburn with Catriona any time and visit me. Talk about the Gorbals being slummy. My God, you've seen nothing until you've seen Cowlairs Pend!"

"The Gorbals isn't slummy," Julie snapped back. "There's plenty of clean, hardworking folk in the Gorbals."

"You'll get a clean, hardworking fist in your eye if you're not careful, hen."

"Send my two across when you're in the Gardens, Madge," Catriona hastily intervened. "It's long past Andrew's bedtime. He'll probably take ages getting used to sleeping in the kitchen with me talking and moving about."

"Och, well, my crowd have survived sleeping in the kitchen so I suppose yours will as well."

The word "survived" brought the night of the air-raid rushing back and she wanted to cry out with the agony of losing baby Robert. Instead she smiled at Madge as she saw her to the door and said:

"As long as they've got a bed, that's the main thing."

"Aye," Madge agreed. "And a roof over their heads. Poor wee buggers, they're entitled to that. I'm glad you managed to get a place, hen. In a real posh part as well! My God, you're fairly coming up in the world, eh? I'd give my right arm to live here but I'm having a hard enough job paying the rent for the dump I'm in." Her freckled face split wide open with laughter and she gave Catriona a nudge before leaving. "You'll have to tell me who owns some of the buildings around here so's I can try giving him the wink!"

Back in the kitchen Julie rolled her eyes.

"What a character!"

"She's terribly kind. Too kind, in fact; that's half Madge's trouble. Look at the stuff she's given me—sheets and pots and pans and dear knows what all. Not to mention the bag of messages she brought today to give me a good start, as she says. She can't afford any of it, you know. It's terrible! You saw me fighting with her, trying to make her take at least some of the stuff back, but she just laughed and wouldn't listen.

"How about a wee cup of tea before the boys come in? You're in no hurry to get away, are you, Julie?"

"No, I told Dad not to wait up for me or anything. He tends to do things like that—worry and fuss a bit since Mammy died."

Catriona put the kettle on and found two cups and saucers in the cupboard beside the fire.

Grief tortured her. She longed for comfort, for Julie to stay the night and not leave her alone. Longing groped desperately this way and that but could not escape the agony in which she nursed her baby in her arms.

"Will I make a bit of toast?" she asked. "It's ages since we've had our tea."

"I know what you're trying to do." Julie smoothed down her skirt and patted her hips. "Sabotage my figure. Jealousy'll get you nowhere, pal."

Catriona laughed.

"Yes, you'd better be careful. Remember what Madge said."

With a roll of her eyes Julie took a couple of slices of bread from the bread tin and put them under the grill.

"Obviously she's not been able to keep her man, and I'm not surprised. Look how she's let herself go. There's no excuse for a woman looking like that. Did you see her streaky leg make-up? And her ankles were filthy. Her hair could have done with a wash, too, and why doesn't she let it grow a bit and put curlers in?"

"Och, she's pregnant, poor soul, and she's already got six children to look after. She's never been too strong either since that last set of twins was born. She had an awful bad time."

Julie deftly turned the toast.

"She looks as strong as a horse. I thought she was going to land one on me. Believe me, pal, I was scared rigid!"

Suddenly they both began to giggle. "If she had socked me, I would have howled," Julie raised her voice in mock distress, "'I'll get my Reggie to you. He's more your size, you dirty big bully!'"

"You and your Reggie!" Catriona shook her head. "You're an awful girl. Watch the toast. You're going to burn it. That'll be the boys at the door! I'll go."

As she went into the small hallway she could hear Julie scraping butter on the bread and singing:

> "There'll be blue-birds over
>     The white cliffs of Dover,
>     Tomorrow, just you wait and see . . ."

Catriona opened the outside door ready to give the boys a row for being late but was taken aback to see Julie's father in the shadows of the landing.

"Mr Gemmell! Come away in. Julie's in the kitchen."

He seemed reluctant to move and hovered uncertainly on the doormat, his eyes evasive in their brown hollows. He looked ill.

"Is something wrong?" Catriona asked.

Dode shuffled into the hall, peeling off his cap.

"Aye. Ah've got bad news."

"Not Reggie!"

"Aye, lass, a telegram!"

"Oh, no!" Catriona wrung her hands. "Oh, no, Mr Gemmell!"

"What am ah going tae say tae her, hen?"

They both listened in anguish to the sound of Julie's happy singing.

Miserably Dode twisted his cap.

"Ah'm nae damnt use."

"You'll just have to give her the telegram. Oh, dear, you'd better go in."

"Dad!" Julie gasped as soon as she saw him. "What are you doing here, you auld rascal?"

She had been eating a bit of toast and she tongued her teeth and flicked crumbs from the corner of her mouth.

"I'm big enough and ugly enough to see myself home. All I need to do is get the subway down the road, for goodness' sake!"

Abruptly Dode produced the telegram and stuffed it into her hands.

"This came. I opened it, lass. Reggie's missing. Failed to return, it says. But don't you worry, hen. He'll have been taken prisoner like Catriona's man."

Julie stared down at the telegram. Her firm cheeks sagged and went grey like an old woman's.

Catriona thought she was going to faint and hurried to put her arms round her and help her into a chair.

"Yes, look how I heard from Melvin. That's what happens, Julie. They get picked up and taken to a camp and eventually the Red Cross or somebody traces them. It's happened lots and lots of times."

"I want to go home, Dad," Julie said.

Dode nodded. He was still twisting his cap and tears shimmered his eyes.

"A damnt shame!"

"Come on."

"Isn't there anything I can do?" Catriona queried, still clinging round the girl's shoulders. "Stay and have a cup of tea. Stay the night if you want to. Both of you. We'll manage."

"No, thanks all the same." Julie became suddenly brisk and rose, tidying down her skirt. "I just want to go home with my dad."

Catriona followed them to the door with short agitated steps.

"Julie, something's just occurred to me. What about Reggie's parents? Shouldn't you go and tell them?"

Julie's face twisted into a travesty of a smile and she ignored Catriona's question.

"Best of luck in your new house, pal. Be seeing you!"

The door banged shut.

Catriona was left helplessly wringing her hands in the empty hall.

# Chapter Twelve

The gate creaked open. Open, then shut again, lazily, like the motion of the trees. The Gardens and the crescent were a green shimmer. Tall trees allowed heavy branches to lean, to undulate, to whisper and ripple.

From where she sat Muriel Vincent could see nothing but gently dancing green framed in the big windows of her sitting-room.

"Pretty as a picture," she had often said. "Such a nice outlook."

The room was quiet, so quiet she was sure she could hear her tiny gold wrist-watch ticking.

The stiff-faced girl in the chair opposite said, "I got these."

She handed over some letters.

The first one had Reggie's squadron and air station address at the top.

Muriel read:

"Dear Mrs Vincent,
Prior to receiving this letter you will have received a telegram informing you that your husband Flight Lieutenant R. Vincent had been reported missing from an operational flight which took place on the night of 6th June 1944.

It is with very deep regret I am writing this letter to convey to you the feelings of the entire squadron following the news that your husband has been reported missing.

On Tuesday evening last an aircraft and crew of which

your husband was pilot and captain took off to carry out a bombing attack on the French coast. This flight was vital and one of the many fighting and courageous efforts called for by the Royal Air Force. The flight should not have taken very long but although other aircraft completed their mission your husband's aircraft failed to return.

The most searching enquiries through all possible channels and organisations have so far revealed nothing but of course it will take some time for possible information to come through from enemy sources and I can only hope your husband and crew are prisoners of war. Meanwhile further information may come available; if so, this will of course be passed to you immediately.

A committee of officers known as a Committee of Adjustment has gathered your husband's personal possessions together and will communicate with you in the near future.

May I again express my personal sympathy in your great anxiety."

The letter was signed by a Wing-Commander.

Another communication, headed "Casualty Branch, Oxford Street, London", began:

"Madam,

I am commanded by the Air Council to express to you their great regret on learning that your husband, Flight Lieutenant Reginald Vincent, Royal Air Force . . ."

The letter from the chaplain was written in a spidery longhand:

"Dear Mrs Vincent,

I am writing to express my profound sorrow that your husband F/Lieut. R. Vincent is missing after operations on the night of 6th June. I understand the uncertainty and anxiety which you must feel. I was up waiting for the crews and it was a great grief to us when your husband's plane failed to return.

I can only hope that your husband and his crew may have escaped disaster by baling out and have become prisoners of war. But of course there is no certainty of this, and it is not until official information comes through via the Red Cross that your terrible suspense will be ended.

You may rest assured that whatever this news, it will be communicated to you at once.

I know that whatever has happened to him he would not have you overcome with sorrow, and you can be sure that his chief thought was less for his own safety than for loyalty and devotion to duty.

Like so many other brave men, he has willingly hazarded his life for a great cause, and we may be proud and thankful for his example.

During these times, we can but commit ourselves and anxieties into the hand of God, who cares and suffers in the griefs of His people.

I pray that you may find in God your comfort and be made strong to bear your heavy load of suffering."

The last letter was neatly typed and signed by a Flight Lieutenant for the Group Captain commanding Reggie's base station:

"Dear Mrs Vincent,

As the officer disposing of the effects of your husband F/Lieut. R. Vincent, may I be permitted to offer you my most sincere sympathy.

In accordance with Air Ministry regulations your husband's personal effects are being forwarded to the RAF Central Depository, Colnbrook, in order that certain formalities may be completed under the provisions of the Regimental Debt Act. All enquiries regarding these effects should be addressed to the Officer Commanding, RAF Central Depository, Colnbrook, Near Slough, Buckinghamshire.

A bicycle, BSA with dynamo and lamp, was found in the effects and is being retained on this station pending disposal instructions from the Central Depository."

Muriel passed each letter in turn to her husband Norman whose face contorted in ugly sobs and had to be hidden and mopped with a handkerchief he fumbled from his trouser pocket. He was shaking all over like an old man.

Muriel viewed him with cold unloving eyes. He had never been any use in a crisis. Oh, he fussed and made cups of tea and insisted on calling in the doctor if she was ill. He could hold on to money, too, and she could depend on the fact that he would never squander all he had and leave them penniless. He did not drink or gamble or go with other women. But he was a weak man.

Long ago she had discovered he was a weak man and she secretly despised him.

She remembered overhearing two women confiding in each other over cups of coffee in a restaurant near Norman's bank. One of them had obviously been having trouble with an overdraft and Norman had taken advantage of her predicament. She was furiously recounting to her friend:

"My dear, he'd always been such a gentleman before. I could hardly believe my ears. You wouldn't speak to me like that, I said, if my Nigel were here! No, my dear, he's no gentleman. He's just a horrid ferret-faced coward!"

Muriel's stare raked over his lanky body, his faded eyes now red with tears, his thin features. Quite a good description she had thought at the time and she still thought so.

The bitterness inside her hardened into a spearhead that aimed straight for Norman's heart. Somehow whatever had happened to Reggie must have been Norman's fault. Norman was a cheat and a failure. He had failed her right from the start. His pathetic inaptitude in bed had sickened her so much she had long since abandoned having anything to do with that side of their marriage.

95

Often she marvelled at Norman's managing to father one child. She thanked God he had managed, of course. Having Reggie, loving him, watching him grow, planning for him, dreaming about the wonderful future he was going to have, had been the only justification for her marriage, for her whole life, in fact.

Nothing Norman could possibly feel would ever match the torture she was in now. Yet he was reduced to blubbering and making a fool of himself in front of the girl. Reggie's wife had more backbone than his father.

In disgust she averted her gaze from Norman. Her eyes wandered over to the window again then came back to the girl sitting opposite.

She stared at the erect figure, immaculate in the black suit and crisp white blouse, hair like polished mahogany, curling neatly inwards and contrasting with creamy skin and hard green eyes.

Reggie loved this girl. Over and over again he had told her, "I love her, Mother. I thought you'd understand. I really love her."

Understanding began to grow in the silent room that had been so familiar to Reggie. How often had he sat in that same chair in which his wife was now sitting.

Muriel cleared her throat.

"I had a letter too. From Reggie. 'In case anything happens to me, Mother', it began. He must have written it at the same time as the one you told us he wrote to you."

Julie raised a brow.

"Oh?"

"He asked us to look after you."

"That won't be necessary. I'm perfectly all right, thank you. Well, if you'll excuse me." She rose, tucking the letters neatly into her handbag and closing it with a snap. "I'd better be going."

Muriel rose too, smiling politely, calmly, yet plummeting down a ski slope of panic as if she would be alone in the world if the girl went away.

"Must you? I . . . I thought perhaps you could stay for dinner. We have plenty, I can assure you."

"No, thank you all the same, but my father's expecting me." Julie turned, hand outstretched to Norman.

"Goodbye, Mr Vincent. Chin up and all that! Reggie wouldn't want you to be upset."

The contrast between the man and the girl was striking. For the first time Muriel saw the proud tilt to Julie's head and thought that there was no danger of her breaking down and acting the fool.

Yet she was only nineteen.

"Mother, will you please take care of her for me", Reggie had written.

She could see him writing the letter just before he went on that last flight, his blond head bent in concentration over the paper. He always wrote in spurts and flourishes with long pauses in between when he thoughtfully chewed his pen.

In the taut silence as Muriel followed her daughter-in-law across the parquet-floored hall, her son felt very near.

At the outside door Julie said jauntily:

"Well, goodbye, Mrs Vincent. Thanks for the afternoon tea."

Just for a second Muriel thought she saw her own anguish mirrored in the green eyes.

She touched the girl's arm.

"You must come again."

"Aye, aw right."

The brittle voice lapsing unexpectedly into broad Glasgow accent gave it a pathetic droop that Muriel found unbearable.

She suddenly ached to take the poor child in her arms and comfort her, but already Julie was away down the stairs, the clumping of her wooden heels filling the stained-glass sanctuary with unaccustomed noise.

Muriel returned hurriedly to the sitting-room and went straight across to peer out of the window.

97

It seemed as if Reggie were at her elbow, all the time anxious.

"*I love her, Mother . . .*"

Recklessly she did something that she would never have dreamed of doing before. She rattled her fist against the window.

Julie jerked round in the crescent below. She gazed up.

Muriel waved.

A stunned look dulled the young features for a moment, then they tightened and brightened. She smiled and waved back.

Muriel watched the girl clip briskly away in the Queen Margaret Drive direction, then turned back into the quiet sitting-room where Norman was still fumbling a handkerchief over his face.

"You ought to be ashamed of yourself." She passed his chair, smoothing the skirt of her dress close to her legs as if it might be contaminated by any contact with him.

Norman shook his head.

"Our only son!"

"Oh, be quiet, Norman. Reggie's all right. Where's your faith? We'll be hearing from him one of these days. It's just a matter of waiting. For his sake, if for nobody else's, try to wait with some dignity."

Norman just kept shaking his head.

"You've always been the same." She picked up the white polo-necked sweater she was knitting for Reggie and tucking the needles under her arms she started them clicking busily.

"Muriel, for pity's sake put that away. I can't bear to see it."

The needles continued as if they were taking pleasure in their jabbing movement.

"Reggie's sweater?"

"Muriel, please!"

"He gets cold. You've heard him say how cold it can get in that bomber."

"He's been shot down."

98

"And taken prisoner."

"Muriel."

"He'll be glad of this in a horrid prisoner-of-war camp. And I'll see that he gets it. I'll contact the Red Cross."

"Our only son!"

"Oh, be quiet. Control yourself. Try to remember you're a man. That girl has more backbone than you. You're always the same, Norman."

"My dear, I'm only facing facts and accepting them. His wife doesn't believe he's alive any more than I do."

"That's a lie. How do you know what she believes? You were so wrapped up in yourself and your own feelings all afternoon you hardly gave the poor girl a glance."

"I couldn't bear to look at her. She reminds me all the time of Reggie. He spoke so much about her that last time he was here. I hope she doesn't come back, Muriel. What's the use, after all?"

"That's so typical of you. It doesn't matter, of course, that Reggie asked us to look after her."

"We'll give her money, see that she never lacks for anything."

"Money! That's all you know about. I've said it before, Norman, and I'll say it again. Thank God Reggie has me. You've never understood him."

Her knitting needles quickened and every now and again she gave a sharp little tug at the ball of white wool.

Norman stood up, crumpling his handkerchief between his hands.

"I understand he's dead."

"Don't say that! You don't know what you're talking about. I keep telling you, Norman, Reggie is alive and well. You're like a poisonous weed. Spreading gloom and depression. Julie must have felt it. You upset her. I could tell. I'm going to see her again as soon as possible and do my very best to reassure her. This dreadful war isn't going to last for ever, I'll tell her. Soon it will be all over and Reggie will be home."

# Chapter Thirteen

D-day, Alec reckoned, had been the beginning of the end. He thanked God for the end but the whole business still sickened him. He could not forget the cost.

Wave upon wave of men, countless British, Canadian, American and all the rest, had been killed and mutilated in the process. Unarmed thousands of civilians had been caught in the centre of the fighting, had clung desperately to their homes and when their houses had been hit by bomb or shell they had run out to crowd together in search of shelter, only to be hit again and again and left to die in the smoking ruins of once serene little cities.

A soldier survivor of a typical battle for a French town had said:

"We won the battle but, considering the high price in American lives, we lost."

It reminded Alec of what he had read of the First World War. From his level, that of the ordinary man being sent in to fight, all wars were the same, just a reckless slaughter. It seemed to him as if some determined top brass had his hand on a tap of human life and turned it on and kept turning it on.

Life gushed out, as easy to come by and as cheap as water, and was swilled just as easily down the drain.

He was so sickened, he felt ashamed to be part of the human race. The top brass, and the politicians, the folk that were supposed to be so much cleverer than the likes of him—with all their brains, their civilisation, their so-called Christianity—was this the only kind of solution they could come up with? Was this the best they could do?

Now the European war was over and he was fortunate enough to be among the first to be released. Some poor mugs had been kept in because they were still needed in the Far East, but he was out, on his own, changed from a number in the Navy to a number in the Labour Exchange, or Buroo as it was known locally.

He had wasted no time in signing on at the Buroo and agitating for work. With a wife and seven weans to keep he could not afford to waste a minute.

As well as taking the precaution of signing on for Buroo money he hurried back to his old office, burst cheerily in, expecting the same old camaraderie; but most of the men he had known were no longer there and he did not even get a decent welcome from the girls. Afterwards, trying to piece together his shattered ego, he decided that they must all have acquired American boy friends with fancy uniforms and plenty of money or men of some other nationality equally glamorous. Compared with a money-flashing Yank or a heel-clicking Polish officer he could see that he would seem dull stuff.

He shrugged them off and wished them luck. As for the men in the office, they were polite and amiable but at the same time surprisingly distant. He felt like a stranger, an uninvited guest who was putting a strain on the party.

The same applied to other men in other offices. He tried to storm quite a few. They were all ticking over very nicely without him. They all had their established routines. They were all fully staffed.

Despite the cheerful bantering bluster that gave energy to his long legs and sent them racing up stairway after stairway, three or four steps at a time, and his fist rat-tat-tat-tat-tatting on prospective employers' doors, he began to feel embarrassed as well as bitter.

"Damn them!" he thought. But his thoughts did not help. Then he told himself: "Early days yet!"

He was barely demobbed and the war in Japan **was not** even over.

Yet he knew that more and more men would be coming home and it would get harder, not easier, to find work.

He kept trying, never letting up because he had always been an active energetic man. Now as well as his natural exuberance he had acquired a new restlessness. It seemed to have been born in the Navy and was tuned to the continuous movement of the ship. It was a kind of impatience that made the tiny overcrowded room and kitchen in Cowlairs Pend close in on him like the bars of a prison.

Worry about money tormented him, too. The over-crowding and the bad condition of the house had affected the children's health. One or the other kept needing the doctor. Fiona coughed all the time and Madge was always dosing her with something.

Day after day he struggled to simulate normality, to ignore his worries. He tried to fit in with the children, be the same overgrown playmate he had once been to them, the loved and respected boss of the Jackson gang. But he found the same strange rejection here as in all the places he visited to ask about work. The gang had closed its ranks. His family resented him. His children had grown into an impertinent, unruly, rebellious mob and his wife had given way to being a slut.

He missed the way it had been before the war when he had been able to take Madge out for treats to cheer her up, when he had been able to burst into the house with an armful of presents for her and the weans. But it went deeper than nostalgia. His inability diminished him.

He tried to talk to Madge, to make half-joking yet desperately serious attempts to explain his feelings, not to mention his money worries to her.

She swatted away his embarrassed gropings as if they were a fly on something she was going to eat.

"Never mind feeling sorry for yourself. Think yourself damned lucky. What about me? I've been stuck in this dump with them wee middens of yours for years. You lumbered me with this lot and even that wasn't enough. You had to have your fun with other women as well. I can't even trust you with my best friends. You're no use. Now you can't even get a job. You that's such a bloody charmer. You that's so clever. You'll be expecting me to go out to work to keep us next and how can I with me still feeding this wee midden."

She indicated their latest, a plump infant of nearly three months, called Charlie, who was energetically sucking at her breast.

"I don't know what we're going to do. I used to trust you. You were my man and I trusted you and somehow that made everything all right." She scratched her lank hair and shoved it behind her ear out of the way. "Now everything's all wrong and I don't know what's going to happen."

He got so fed up, he escaped to the pub and drank himself stupid a couple of times. He took the whole width of the Pend, bouncing off one side, staggering across the cobbles and bouncing off the other on his way home, and on his arrival he immediately tried to force himself on everyone in a desperate effort to ingratiate himself in their affections. Nothing but bedlam resulted. The older weans had shaken free of him, loudly sneering in disgust, "Get off!" and the younger ones had screamed and sobbed and yelled:

"Mammy, Mammy!"

Afterwards he felt guilty and ashamed, not only of worsening relations with his children but because he knew he could not afford to drink.

He was also angry at himself for giving Madge something else to nag about.

Fortunately, his inborn Glasgow humour kept coming to his rescue and sometimes Madge had to laugh in spite of herself.

"Have a heart, hen," he'd say. "I admit I'm an unemployed rapist but don't tell me I'm a hopeless wino as well!"

Sometimes they would chat together almost like normal and Madge would tell him all the gossip.

"Catriona MacNair's man's coming back. She heard the other day and she's in a right flap. He's been a prisoner of war, poor bugger. Still, he's lucky compared with some. You haven't met Catriona's pal, the one she used to work with, have you? Julie Vincent, a bit of a haughty piece but quite a nice wee lassie all the same, comes from the Gorbals. Catriona and her used to work in Morton's in Buchanan Street. Well, her man was shot down on D-day. It's the queerest thing that, Alec."

"Queer? Being shot down? My God, hen, if you'd seen as many shot down as I've seen . . ."

"No, no," she interrupted impatiently. "Julie's mother-in-law."

He laughed and shook his head.

"Women! I don't know what you're talking about, hen."

"Catriona says Mrs Vincent wouldn't have anything to do with Julie at first. Then Reggie—that's Julie's man—got shot down and from that moment Julie's never been able to get Mrs Vincent off her back!"

"You're sure it wasn't Mr Vincent Catriona said?"

"Don't be filthy. Trust you to make a joke of the poor lassie's trouble. You don't care a damn about anybody."

"I'm sorry, hen. I'm sorry!" He hastened to veer her back into the path of good humour. "You mean Julie's man was killed?"

"They weren't sure at first but word came through that he was dead not long after he was posted missing. Och, that was a while ago now. Must be a year or more. Aye, he went missing on D-day. But that's queer about her mother-in-law, isn't it? Catriona says it's fair tormenting Julie."

"She's probably at the change of life. Remember Ma went a bit queer?"

"Aye, poor soul. My God, if it's not one thing it's another. Women just get free of bringing up weans and then they've 'the change' to suffer."

"Well, I never invented it, hen." He laughed, then realised too late that in laughing he had blundered.

"Aye, laugh, laugh!" Madge shouted in his face. "It's a great joke for the likes of you. As long as you're getting your f——ing way, you've nothing to worry about!"

"Madge, the weans!" he pleaded. "They'll be talking like that next."

She laughed bitter, ugly laughter.

"Oh, listen to Saint Alec. I was just stating a plain fact in plain words." She shook her head. "I wouldn't have cared, Alec. I would have struggled along being pregnant all the time, being trauchled and tired and mixed up and not being able to manage and I still would have been quite content and happy if I'd thought you cared."

He groaned.

"But, hen. I do care. My God, you go on like a gramophone record. You've got an absolute obsession, Madge. It's really getting terrible."

"I've got an obsession? I've never lied to you. I've never . . ."

"Oh, shut up!"

He couldn't help it. It was just impossible to sit quietly listening to another long spiel about his heinous infidelities and in his rush to get up and escape he stumbled over Charlie who was sitting on the floor with a dummy teat stuck in his mouth. The dummy teat spurted out to dangle on its yellow cord and Charlie let out a scream of protest.

Madge hauled herself up.

"You kicked that wee wean, you dirty big coward!"

"I did not!"

Madge's red shovels of hands punched out wildly and in desperation he gripped her by the wrists.

"You're mad!"

"If I'm mad it's you that's made me."

Her freckles were ugly brown blotches on an unhealthy grey skin and her eyes strained huge and wild with anger.

"See him! See him!" she shouted round at the now screaming children. "See what a rotten midden you've got for a daddy!"

To Alec, this was the last straw. He flung her wrists aside.

"You're a great help," he said bitterly. "A great help. Well, you might as well know it all and really get to work on me. The rent's so much in arrears now we'll never be able to make up the money. You said you didn't know what we're going to do. Well, I don't know what we're going to do either." His voice broke. "The way things look I'm going to be in the jail and you and the weans in Barnhill."

The screaming and sobbing of all the children lifted to a crescendo at the mention of the word Barnhill. They all knew it was the poorhouse.

"Shut up!" Madge bawled above them. "And get away through to the room, the whole crowd of you. Charlie and all. Haul him out along with you."

Alec lit a cigarette and thought bitterly of how any time now everybody would be celebrating VJ-day. The end of the war. What they had all been fighting for. Freedom. Victory. A decent way of life. What a joke!

As soon as the kitchen was empty and quiet, Madge faced him.

"What are you talking about us all getting separated for? You're my man and we're your family."

"I know, hen. But with these doctor's bills and the medicines and one thing and another ... You must have seen it coming yourself. We've been robbing Peter to pay Paul."

"They'll try and sell all our furniture, all our things, everything we've got, Alec." She gripped the back of a chair for support. "They'll try and separate us."

He grabbed her angrily into his arms.

"If I could just get a bloody job. I'm going back down to that Buroo again. I'll plead with them. To hell with collar-and-tie jobs and offices, hen. I'll empty bins. I'll sweep the streets. I'll do anything."

"What if they don't have anything? The rotten middens haven't had anything so far."

"We'll just have to do a moonlight." His handsome face, already fatigued and embittered by war, now creased with worry. "But where we'll go I've no idea. Who'd take us in, with all our mob! How will we even get a lorry or something to move all our things?"

Madge thought for a minute.

"I know!"

"What, hen?"

"The MacNairs still have their bread van somewhere. That'll do fine. And see over the West End where she lives, Alec, there's big houses lying empty. It's wicked. Why should there be houses lying empty and weans needing a roof over their heads? Some squatters have moved into one already. We could go there too."

"Oh, just a minute, hen. I don't know if I agree with squatters. Everybody can't just go about taking everything they want!"

She pushed him roughly away.

"You're a fine one to talk! It's all right when it's taking a woman you want, is it? But it's different when it's taking a place for your wife and weans?"

"All right, all right." He groaned. "But don't you see, Madge, it's illegal. They'll have me in the end."

"No, they won't. They won't." She brandished her big fists but he could see that she was trembling. "Nobody's going to take you away from me again. I won't let them. Do you hear, you dirty big midden? I won't let them!"

"Och, Madge!" He took her in his arms again. "If it's what you want, hen, we'll go right away."

He shut his eyes and tried to blot out the terrible picture of chairs and rolls of linoleum and cots and brushes and mattresses and all the pathetic paraphernalia that they had collected over the years, not to mention the weans, all being crammed into an old bread van in the middle of the night and setting off rootless and defenceless yet still dependent on him, to he knew not where.

"I'll go and see Catriona," he said.

"*I'll* go and see Catriona," Madge corrected. "You stay here and look after the weans."

"But this house out her way . . . I'll have to know exactly where, won't I?"

"We'll all go then." She swung round towards the door and blasted it with an enormous yell. "Sadie! Agnes! Hector! William! Fiona! Maisie! Come back through here at once, and bring Charlie!"

# Chapter Fourteen

"I can't eat it!" Melvin's red-rimmed eyes glared down at the large chocolate cake. Brown crumbs speckled his moustache proving that he had tried. His mouth warped with bitterness.

"But, Melvin, I thought you said you'd been dreaming about a chocolate cake for years. Don't worry about rations or anything. I'll manage. Eat it, Melvin. It's all yours. I made it specially."

"I can't eat it, you fool. My belly's shrunk!"

"Oh, dear!"

This was yet another problem Melvin had brought home. During the day he could not eat and at night he could not sleep. The cavity bed had been out of the question.

"I'm not going to sleep in that hole in the wall." He had swung away in an effort to hide the apprehension in his face but she had seen it and been moved to put her arms round him and comfort him like a child.

"It's all right, dear."

He pushed her side with a bluster of bravado.

"I could if I wanted to. I don't choose to, that's all. It's space I want now. Space to breathe and stretch myself."

"Yes, all right, Melvin, but what can we do? There's no place else. Except the floor."

"Well, what's wrong with that? It's only a temporary measure. I've got plans, big plans."

So she had pushed back the table and chairs and made up a bed as best she could on the kitchen floor. She crept in first and watched with a mixture of fear and compassion as he undressed to reveal the skeleton of the man he had once been. Yet he still had plenty of swagger.

"I've got about five years' pay lying. Think of that!"

"That's lovely!"

"And I had a few pounds stacked away before that."

"Fancy!"

"I'm going to speak to Da, get things moving about a new business." He hitched big bony shoulders inside his pyjamas. "You can't keep a good man down!"

"No, dear."

She strained up to peer at his grey hair, his sallow face deeply carved with lines, before crumpling back with her feelings in disorder. He was an old man. An old man scratching himself and stomping over to come and lie beside her. She wished she could pluck herself out of the room and throw herself to the winds. She had crazy visions, rapid jerky pictures of herself escaping, being free, starting life again.

But there were the children. Her stomach contracted with immediate fear at the thought, no matter how fleeting, of leaving them.

Melvin's lovemaking touched a need inside her, yet at the same time it flared up a disgust of herself. She turned away afterwards and tried to blot herself out in sleep but Melvin kept his hand between her legs and refused to stop fondling her. For hours she lay unable to sleep, fatigue and the invasion of her privacy irking her beyond measure. The thought that even if she did sleep, he would still be "using" her seemed to take away any last vestige of pretence that she had ever been or would ever be a free human being with dignity or rights of her own.

Resentment and anger simmered in a cauldron of repressed emotion. But he had suffered years in a prison camp, she kept reminding herself, and because of this she kept forcing herself to be patient and to please him.

She had baked the chocolate cake to please him and he had taken one half-hearted nibble at it and then put it down.

Fergus and Andrew were at the table, too, waiting eagerly, eyes on the cake, mouths drooling. Then Fergus kicked Andrew under the table and Andrew reacted obediently to cue.

"Can I have a bit then?"

Melvin's reaction was so violent it startled all of them, including old Duncan who had been chomping noisily at a crust of bread with his too-loose dentures.

"Leave that cake alone, you ugly fat little bastard!" His voice was not loud yet it shook the air with venom. "You've enough fat on you to keep you going for years. Mummy's spoiled brat, aren't you? Mummy's plump wee cuddles?"

Andrew's eyes stretched enormous in a face gone white. His lips trembled but he did not utter a sound.

Catriona was outraged.

"What are you picking on him for? Fergus wants a bit too. He's too fly to ask, that's all."

"Yes, Fatso's always been your favourite. I wonder why?"

"Have you gone mad or something?" Catriona got up from the table, ready to bodily protect Andrew if necessary. "What does it matter about the stupid chocolate cake. You said you didn't want it."

"I didn't say I didn't want it but, oh, let him have it. Let him have it. All of you have a bit. Eat it all. Don't worry about me!"

Catriona sat down again. Lack of sleep plus the new irritations of the day had started pain pressing in at her temples. "You mean you might eat it afterwards? Well, that's all right then. I'm sorry, boys, but I made the cake for Daddy and he might . . ."

"No . . . no!" Melvin interrupted, pushing the cake into the centre of the table with a grand gesture. "Eat it! Eat it! Don't worry about me!"

"But, Melvin . . ."

"Eat it!"

In miserable silence the children pushed pieces of chocolate cake into their mouths.

Eventually Melvin said:

"We're getting out of this place for a start."

"It's nice here," Catriona muttered resentfully. "In a nice close, in a nice district. The children play across in the Botanic Gardens."

She wished he had never come back. She had been content pottering about on her own as if she were a little girl again playing at houses. There was a cosiness about the new place and it gave her a sense of achievement to look at it and realise that she had found it, paid the deposit and negotiated everything herself.

It was a bit cramped with her father-in-law in the room and Fergus kept harassing her with objections about having to sleep with the old man. Still, at night once they were settled and Andrew tucked in the kitchen bed and the fire was flickering, a glow of security and real pleasure warmed her. There was a kind of happiness in busying herself doing odd jobs, or gazing out the window at life ebbing back and forth in Byres Road.

Sometimes she curled up beside the fire and read a book. Sometimes she crept in beside Andrew and enjoyed a read in bed. Every now and again she stole a thrill by gently touching the little boy as he slept, caressing his hair with her fingertips, or the childish contours of his face. Or she would lie for a long time holding his hand.

"This kitchen's not much bigger than the bedspace I had to live in in the prison camp and not nearly so tidy or well organised. I never could stand poky disorganised places. I always had a house to be proud of and that's what I'm going to have again."

"I suppose that means I'm going to be a slave to the polishing cloth like I was before. I don't understand you."

"You wouldn't know a good polish if you saw it. You should have seen the shine on my floors when my Betty was alive."

Catriona rose and began to gather up the dirty dishes.

"Oh, for pity's sake, we're not going to go over all that again. I had enough of your marvellous Betty years ago."

"Don't you dare talk to me like that." His voice never rose but the menace in it was unmistakable. Duncan shuffled to his feet.

"I'm away to the room, son. Maybe there's something good on the wireless."

"I'll come through and talk to you later. We'll have to get another business."

Old MacNair scratched his beard.

"Aye, I know, but it's easier said than done. There's businesses to be bought, oh, aye. There's old Russell. I meet him often across in the Gardens and we have a blether and a smoke on one of the seats. He was telling me he's thinking of retiring. He's got a place just down the road. Been here for years. But there's all the bother about allocations. You've got to have allocations in the district. Our allocations were for Clydend."

"We could soon swing the allocations. What's to stop us paying a few hundred extra for 'goodwill'?"

"Not having a few extra hundred," Duncan replied tartly. "That's what could stop us. I'm away through to the room."

"He's got it all right and plenty to spare," Melvin growled after the old man had left. "He's made thousands. I've done his books and I know. For years I worked for that old skinflint for no more than pocket money. He took me out of school and paid me a few bob for working like a slave. It was like drawing blood out of a stone to eventually get a decent wage off him and for that I ran his business. He's been no bloody use for years. This time I'm going to see that I get a partnership."

"Do you think you'll get him to agree? It is his money."

Melvin's eyes bulged.

"Are you deaf as well as stupid? I've just been telling

you how I earned that money. I slaved for it for him and I took him into my home so that he didn't need to pay for his house and all his expenses. He's going to be fed and looked after for the rest of his life, thanks to what I've done."

"Yes, and you never as much as mentioned it to me."

"What do you mean, mentioned it to you?"

"You never said a word to me until after it was all settled and I'm the one who's got all the work and worry."

"You!" he sneered. "What work have you ever done? What worry have you ever had?"

She turned away and put the dishes in the sink. She could not bear the pain of saying—my baby is dead.

"Nothing! Nothing! My life's been just dandy since I met you!"

"Yes, well remember that," he warned, taking her seriously. "What's the top-notch houses round about here? The really best ones you've set eyes on?"

"Houses?"

"That's what I said."

"Why?"

"Just answer my question."

The children began to argue in the background and she recognised the pattern of sound. Fergus was tormenting Andrew about something and at any minute Andrew was either going to erupt into violence and pitch himself bodily at Fergus or burst into noisy tears of frustration.

"Away out and play, boys. Fergus, here's money for sweets." She smiled, hoping to bribe him into a better humour. "And there's some coupons in this book. Share them with Andrew and take his hand crossing the road. He's only a wee boy and I'm depending on you to look after him."

Immediately the words were out she worried about whether she ought to have mentioned about taking Andrew's hand and looking after him in case it revealed any preference for Andrew and incurred any further jealousy or displeasure.

She tried to console herself by thinking that surely it was natural for every mother to feel a special kind of love for her youngest, her baby. Then pain so terrible that nothing in the world could ever soothe away took possession of her. She could feel the milky-smelling softness of Robert in her arms, see his round eyes drugged with sleep and adoration as she nursed him and sung to him.

> *I left my baby lying there,*
> *Oh, lying there, oh, lying there,*
> *I left my baby lying there,*
> *When I returned my baby was gone . . .*

She pressed her hand against her mouth.

"The houses! The houses!" Melvin insisted.

"What houses?"

"Jumpin' Jesus, wake up!"

"Och, there's lots of nice places round about here. The West End's full of nice places. Where Julie's in-laws live is nice. Julie's a girl I used to work with. She took me round there one day."

"Round where?"

"Her mother-in-law lives in a big red sandstone flat facing the river at the other side of the Botanic Gardens."

"Show me!"

"Now?"

"Now!"

"I'm doing the dishes."

"Now, I said."

"Oh, for goodness' sake!'

"For goodness' sake," he mimicked. "What do you know about goodness? I don't believe that last brat was mine."

The unexpectedness of his words rocked her. She clutched on the sink for support.

"Melvin, please, you don't know how I feel."

"I'm not so sure about Fatso, either!"

"You don't know what you're saying."

"I could get rid of you, you know. You think yourself damned lucky. I'm doing you a big favour keeping you on. But just watch it. Watch it! What are you standing there for, then? You look as if you're going to puke in the sink. Hurry up!"

"Is this how it's going to be?"

"What do you mean, 'Is this how it's going to be'?"

"Are you going to torment me all the time and make my life a misery?"

He guffawed with laughter and shot big hands out to fondle her breasts and make her immediately shrink away from the window.

"Somebody might see!"

"You love it, don't you!"

Shrivelled miserably into a corner, her hands and arms twisting in an effort to protect herself, she said:

"I thought you wanted to go out."

"Sure! Sure! Get your coat."

He tugged at his tie and buttoned the jacket of his demob suit, a crumpled navy-blue pin-stripe that nipped in at the waist.

Outside, striding along Byres Road and across into Queen Margaret Drive the breeze flapped the trousers of the suit against his bones and sunlight made shadows hollow his face. Darting a look up at him she wondered what he was thinking as he marched along, his moustache puffing up and his thin hair feathering.

Was he dreaming grand dreams of a house without cavity beds? Did he expect one in Mrs Vincent's building to be empty, ready and waiting for him to command?

She sighed and took his arm.

"Was it terrible for you in the prison camp, Melvin?"

"Och, I was hardly ever in a camp," he scoffed. "I was escaping all the time. Nobody could get the better of me. They couldn't pin me down, not even the Gestapo. It's a fine place here, right enough." He took big breaths as they went over the Queen Margaret bridge. "A lot different

116

from Dessie Street. Remember all the dust and noise? The yards across the main road and the street all lumpy with cobbles?"

She made no reply.

"This is the place, all right." He gazed around, puffing out his chest. "Fit for a king!"

"Round to the left," she said, then after a minute or two: "This is Botanic Crescent."

He stopped and stared at the big three-storied terrace houses until she became embarrassed and tugged at his arm.

"People will see us. Come on, Melvin. The tenements are at the other end but don't hang about there either. Julie's mother-in-law might notice."

He began marching along at such a cracking pace she was harassed into taking little running steps to keep up with him.

On an impulse she nearly blurted out the news of how quite a few of the houses in the West End had been invaded by squatters and only the other day Madge and Alec had installed themselves in a place already occupied by a crowd of other families. She had since heard they had barricaded themselves in and the police and other officials were trying to evict them. However, fear of mentioning Alec's name in case it might arouse Melvin's suspicions held the words in check just in time.

"Oh, yes!" Melvin eyed the tenement building with satisfaction when they reached the other end of the crescent. "Very nice! Very nice indeed! Come on, which close is hers?"

"Why?"

"If there's any houses going around here, she's the one to know, stupid. She's on the spot, isn't she?"

"I've only met the woman once. Oh, I don't like it. Come on home, Melvin, please!"

"Don't be stupid. My God, if I left everything to you, where would we be?"

"I found a nice wee place."

"Look, it's obvious from here that those are lovely big flats. There's no comparison with the likes of this and that poky wee hole you call a house. Which close is hers?"

She led him up Mrs Vincent's close, her flaxen head lowered.

"This is ridiculous!"

"What do you mean—'This is ridiculous'?"

Over-awed by the dignified silence of the tiled close and church-like windows of the landing, both their voices lowered to hissing whispers.

"I've only met the woman once. What'll she think?"

"What do you mean—'What'll she think'?"

"For goodness' sake!"

When they reached Mrs Vincent's door which was half stained glass and half polished oak, Melvin immediately pulled the bell but he nudged Catriona and said:

"You do the talking."

She glanced up at him, her irritation mixed with surprise. She thought she detected a tremble in his voice.

The door opened to reveal a petite well-preserved woman with black hair, a flawless skin and a beautiful fragrance around her.

"Yes?" Her eyes were expressionless but the slight raising of her brow and tilting of her head indicated a polite interest, a willingness to listen.

"I'm a friend of Julie's," Catriona began and once started, desperation forced her to race along in a performance of smiling confidence. "Catriona MacNair. We have met once but you probably won't remember. This is my husband, Melvin. I hope you don't mind us coming to your door like this but we wondered if you might be able to help us."

"Perhaps you had better come in." Mrs Vincent stood aside and allowed them to enter the hall. Then she led them to the sitting-room.

"We have a very small room and kitchen flat in Byres

Road." Catriona kept the smile stuck to her face. "And we're looking for larger accommodation. Now that my husband's home we're rather overcrowded. Melvin's been in a prisoner-of-war camp in Germany."

She saw the pain flit across the other woman's eyes and she hated Melvin for bringing her here and making her hurt Mrs Vincent. She wished she could break through the invisible barriers that separated one human being from another. She longed to say, "I lost a son too. I know how you feel." Instead her soft voice kept lightly, breathlessly chattering.

"This area is very nice and we were wondering if you might know of any flats here that are likely to become vacant in the near future. My husband was just saying—someone on the spot is the best person to know about these things."

"Do sit down!"

They accepted her invitation and perched themselves side by side on the edge of the settee and waited tensely in the silence that followed.

"I'm so sorry to bother you, Mrs Vincent." Catriona's words tickled the perfumed air again. "It's not fair of us to be putting you to any trouble."

"Not at all. I'd like to help. But I'm afraid . . ." Mrs Vincent lapsed into silence for another few minutes. "I simply cannot think of any flats around here that are liable to be for sale. I'm sorry. The only thing I can suggest is that you keep watching the *Glasgow Herald*. You might see something suitable advertised and I'll certainly pass on anything I hear from any of the neighbours."

"That's terribly kind of you. I'll give you our address."

"No," Mrs Vincent said hastily. "Please don't bother. I can always see Julie and tell her." She turned to Melvin. "Were you in the RAF, Mr MacNair?"

"No," Melvin said. "The Army."

"My son was killed over France." She blinked across at the mantelpiece. "That's his photograph."

"A fine-looking lad." Melvin bounced up to go over and take a closer look.

"Yes, he was always very good-looking even as a child. I have some other photographs here." She reached for her handbag and lowered her head as she fingered through its contents.

"That's him when he was seven and here's another taken when we were on holiday at Dunoon." She passed around one photograph after another and both Melvin and Catriona admired each in turn.

All the time Catriona was telling herself she had no pictures of Robert, no clothes, no trace. One day the memory of his face she cherished in her mind might fade away and she would have nothing.

At last they rose to go, politely refusing the cup of tea they were offered.

"I'm sorry I haven't been of much help," Mrs Vincent murmured as she showed them out. "The only place I know of that's going to be on the market soon is the big terrace house next to my mother's at the other end of the crescent. The old lady who lived there fell and broke her hip. She's been in hospital for a long time now. She'll never be able to come back and look after herself again. They've moved her to a home and her solicitor is attending to the sale of her house. But I don't suppose that would be of any interest to you. I must see Julie and tell her you called."

The door was barely closed when Melvin whispered excitedly:

"Fate, that's what it is! I was admiring these terrace houses on the way here. '*That's* what I call a spacious house,' I said to myself. 'That's the kind of place anybody would be proud of.' Come on, we'll have another look."

She could hardly believe her ears.

"You can't be serious."

"It's fate, I tell you."

"Melvin, they're huge. Don't be ridiculous. They've

got three stories not counting the attics and cellars. We couldn't possibly keep a house like that. Julie says Reggie's grandmother has money of her own. They've got a living-in servant and a daily char."

Melvin hitched back his shoulders.

"Maybe one day I'll be able to employ servants too. I'm not going to be content with a small bakery business this time. I'm going to build up something really big. MacNair is going to be a household word before I'm through. And I'm going to have that house. And it's going to be like a palace."

"You're away in a world of dreams," Catriona said.

# Chapter Fifteen

Julie's greatest fear was that the letter would disintegrate or in some way vanish. She opened it tenderly and read it. She had already consumed every word a hundred times or more.

"My own dearest wife,
   You'll probably never receive this. I certainly hope you don't.
   I just thought I'd dash off a few words in case I 'failed to return'—as they say.
   Well, I've always returned so far and I've more reason than ever to come back now that you're waiting for me.
   I keep thinking what a lucky chap I am. Wasn't it a stroke of luck you liked Felix Mendleson's Hawaiian Band and went to hear him that night at Green's Playhouse? I thank my lucky stars over and over again that I decided to go there that night too.
   It was the merest chance, darling. I sweat every time I think of it but I nearly went to the Locarno.
   I might never have seen you standing there in front of one of the pillars with your head in the air and that perky look that seemed a kind of challenge. I might never have felt the smoothness of your skin, sweet talcum-smelling like a baby's. I might never have shared those precious private moments when you gave yourself to me with such loving generosity.
   I couldn't bring myself to say this to you in person, darling, and probably I'll always be too embarrassed to say the words to your face, but—thank you for loving me.

I love you, Julie.

But, my own dear, proud little brand-new wife, if anything should happen to me tonight, don't spend the rest of your life thinking about me and what might have been. You're too young for that.

I want you to be cherished and looked after. I want you to be happy. I want you to have a lifetime of love and happiness.

From your adoring husband,

Reggie."

She folded the letter away in her handbag. She did not know what to do. She lit a cigarette and watched her father briskly splash water on his face then attack it with a towel. He was getting ready to go out again.

"Everybody's acting like they want me fur their best pal the day, hen." He rubbed his hands and did a little joyous shuffle. "I've had that many laughs and blethers wi' folk ma head's spinning."

"I know what's making your head spin. You don't fool me, you auld rascal. When you come in tonight—it's straight through to the room with you, do your hear? Don't you dare come staggering into this kitchen wakening me with any of your drunken chatter."

"You're no' staying in, are ye, hen?"

"I don't know what I'm going to do. I'll probably go over to Catriona's. Away you go and don't worry about me."

She turned away stretching lazily, as if she had not a care in the world.

"Cheerio then, hen. Try and enjoy yersel'."

"Aye, aw right. Cheerio, Dad."

She took a deep drag at her cigarette then tossed it into the fire.

She stared at herself in the mantelpiece mirror. There she was. Dark glossy hair. Milky skin. Emerald eyes. Not bad-looking. Good figure. Twenty years of age. Widow. Widow about to celebrate Victory day.

What victory?

She lit another cigarette and went out still smoking it. Her mother-in-law would not approve of that. Smoking in the street. Tut tut. Not that she would criticise. She was too much of a lady for that but she might gently advise or exude that aura of ladylike suffering that made it only too obvious you were offending her sensibilities.

She wished Mrs Vincent would leave her alone, get off her back, forget she had ever existed. It was a strain never knowing when she would pop into the shop and invite her in that casual but determined way to lunch in MacDonald's or Wylie & Lochead's. Or phone the shop with an invitation to Kelvinside to see about something or other. Letters often arrived asking the same questions or, worse, just anxiously enquiring about her health.

Shaking Mrs Vincent off had proved impossible for more reasons than one. Julie had tried. Over and over again she had made promises to call at Kelvinside and then never turned up. It only made the situation worse. Her mother-in-law rushed to contact her again to make sure that everything was all right. She refused to take offence and never stopped pressing invitations and presents on her.

Julie knew how she felt. It was not that Mrs Vincent cared about her. Her son was all that had ever mattered and in his wife she somehow saw her last link with him.

Often Julie felt the same way. Occasionally loneliness overcame her and she went to visit the Vincents of her own free will. Always she regretted it. If Mr Vincent was there she felt out on a limb, lonelier than ever, isolated in that special kind of severance peculiar to widows. The pain of this could flare into agonising proportions by just being in the company of a married couple, even though the married couple's relationship was far from perfect. They still had a relationship. They were a pair. They could fight together, gossip together, eat together, sleep together.

She was neither one thing nor the other. She was no longer the single, carefree, uninitiated girl she had once been. Oceans of sadness cut her off from single girls. Yet she was not married like married women either. Night after night in bed she fevered to have her husband by her side and this physical agony was only a small part of a world of grief at losing him.

If Mrs Vincent was alone the visit was no happier. There would be the torment of seeing Reggie's photos and hearing all about his exploits as a child. They spoke about him nearly all the time. It was terrible.

There seemed so much of Reggie's life she had never shared. She wanted to see the photographs, to touch his cricket bat and his old school bag, and his favourite books, to sit on the chairs he had sat on, to hold close to her the clothes he had worn.

Yet it was terrible. She avoided going to Kelvinside as much as she could.

Tonight she felt compelled to go somewhere and her conscience nagged at her that it might be a kindness to visit Mrs Vincent. Walking smartly round to Bridge Street to catch the subway, she tried to be sensible, to fight the strange horror rising inside her. Maybe she would drop in for a few minutes after visiting Catriona.

Visits to Catriona were different now. Her husband had returned and Catriona was obsessed by all the apparent worries this entailed. They were in the throes of buying some ridiculously big house and Catriona did not know how she would ever be able to clean and polish it all.

She had shrugged and told Catriona:

"Well, don't."

But she envied Catriona her trouble with her house and her husband, her planning, her worrying, all her homely harassments.

It was obvious when she arrived at Byres Road and Catriona opened the door that she had been weeping. Her hazel eyes were inflamed and her face looked hot and blotchy.

"Oh, come in, Julie. It's nice to see you." Her voice

shrivelled to a whisper. "He's got this business and he's wanting me to manage the shop as well. Did you ever hear anything so ridiculous? The house has ten rooms counting the attics. I don't how how I'm going to manage that."

Before Julie reached the kitchen and entered the family circle she already felt out of it, an intruder. Before she was inside, she itched to escape. To be a non-participator, an observer, meant spending the rest of the evening smiling hypocritically on an icy fringe. It was unendurable.

"I've only dropped in for a minute. I thought I might say hello to the old ma-in-law and then scamper off to join the celebrations in George Square. Aren't you lot going?"

Catriona darted an uncertain look at Melvin.

"Actually, I wanted to take some things to Madge."

"Of course we're going. This is VJ night." Melvin allowed his words to puff out in between sucking at the pipe he kept gripped firmly between his teeth. "The police pipe band's going to be playing in George Square and the City Chambers is going to be floodlit and they've got fairy-lights in all the trees. I knew we'd win in the end."

"I've these things to take to Madge first, Melvin. I won't be long."

"What do you mean, you won't be long? She lives in Springburn!"

"No, they're squatters now. They're in a house over in Huntley Gardens."

"Squatters?" Melvin aimed his pipe at her as if it were a gun. "You wash your hands of them. No wife of mine is going to get mixed up with that mob. A crowd of right no-users."

The red blotches on Catriona's face merged into a scarlet flush.

"Nobody's ever any use as far as you're concerned. You always seem to see the worst in people. Well, Madge helped me when I needed it and I'm going to help her now."

"O.K. O.K." Julie laughed. "Call it a draw, pals. I'll deliver the goods. Where are they?"

Catriona hesitated, taken aback by the offer as if she had forgotten Julie existed.

"That's very kind of you, Julie, but I shouldn't ask you."

"You're not asking me." Shrugging, she lit a cigarette. "I'm at a loose end. It'll give me something to do."

"It's just some food and odds and ends in this basket. Well, all right but stay and have a cup of tea first."

"No, thanks all the same but I'd rather be off." She lifted the basket. "Take it easy, pals. The war's over, remember."

Catriona followed her apologetically out to the hall.

"I'm sorry you're having to rush away, Julie. Come again soon and stay for a meal." Her voice contracted into a hiss. "Isn't he terrible? You know where it is, don't you? Cross the road and . . ."

"Stop worrying!" Julie laughed, but returning back down the stairs she kept swallowing at the lump in her throat. It would have been different if Catriona had been on her own. They could have spent the evening giggling and gossiping together. It would have been company and something to do.

She flicked her cigarette into the gutter when she reached the street and crossed the road with quick capable steps. At the other side she glanced round to see if Catriona had come to the window as usual to give her a wave. The window was empty. Catriona would have completely forgotten her and returned to the absorbing world of conflict that she and her husband shared.

At the sedate little backwater called Huntley Gardens, in a terraced house thundering with the noise of children's feet on bare floorboards and vibrating at fever pitch with the racket of voices, Julie had the same experience of being alone, on the outside of a world shared by absorbed, together people, a world in which she belonged, yet had no longer any place.

127

Madge's husband invited her in and introduced himself as Alec. He was tall and broad-shouldered and had a tanned face with dark, sexy eyes that immediately awakened with appreciation when he saw her. He held out his hands.

"If you're a policewoman come to arrest me, I'll come quietly, hen, but you'd be safer if you put the handcuffs on!"

She chuckled.

"Do I look like a policewoman?"

"You look gorgeous!"

Madge came striding into the hall then with a baby hanging on her hip, its mouth plugged with a dummy teat and its legs wide like a frog's.

"What do you want?" she asked, tucking her straggly hair behind her ears and at the same time hoisting up the slithering baby.

Julie held out the basket.

"Not a thing, pal. Not a thing. These are from Catriona."

"Och, she's a good wee soul, isn't she?" Madge was slightly abashed. "I'm sorry I can't ask you to stay for a cup of tea, hen. There's God knows how many other families here and only one cooker." She erupted in a bluster of laughter that jerked the baby off his perch on her hip again. She hauled him back up. "It's hellish, sure it is, Alec."

"You're not kidding!" Alec groaned. "And it'll get worse, not better. They say they're going to turn off the water and electricity."

"Och, we'll manage somehow."

"But, Madge, hen, I keep telling you . . ."

"I know what you keep telling me . . ."

"But we've got to face facts sooner or later."

"We're facing facts now but we're facing them together and that's how it should be!"

"Excuse me, pals, I'll have to go. I'm off to George Square to join in the wild celebrations and all that," Julie interrupted. "I hope you manage all right, Madge. I'll be hearing from Catriona how you get on."

Back outside again, she walked smartly yet without paying any attention to direction. She was away down Byres Road before she could see through her mist of wretchedness. It had been her intention to pay Mrs Vincent a visit and then take the blue tram into town. Her heels went off beat, slowed a little, made to turn, then stopped. She knew she would not be able to bear the Vincents tonight. Yet she longed to make some contact, some sort of communion with Reggie.

University Avenue led off Byres Road and on impulse she started walking quickly along it until she reached the grey spired and turreted university building, then she went straight in unchallenged with her shoulders back and her head in the air.

Some young men wearing long university scarves came down the steps of one of the buildings. She wondered if they realised how lucky they were. The war was over. They would have a chance to live. She turned away from the building and gazed at the magnificent view of Glasgow stretched out underneath as far as the eye could see, from the hill she was standing on to the far hills in the distance.

Down to the right beyond fat green banks of trees was Kelvin Park and the art galleries. To the left, high on the horizon rose the elegant ring of terraced houses called Park Circus. Hidden by more trees but on a map looking like the tiers of a wedding cake, were the other beautiful terraces, some of the many examples of Glasgow's fine architecture.

Reggie had loved Glasgow, too. He had been much more knowledgeable about it than her, of course. She remembered one day he had taken her on a tour of the city. Buildings she had passed every day, places she had known all her life had taken on new meaning and interest. Hand in hand they stopped and stared and gazed up as he told her little anecdotes about the history of different places.

She had never been in Glasgow Cathedral until that day when Reggie had taken her and she remembered how she

had enjoyed him quoting Zachary Boyd who had once
been bishop in the cathedral and who had fancied himself
as a poet. Apparently Zachary Boyd had left his money
to the university on condition that they published his
poetry. The university had taken the money but could
never bring themselves to fulfil the condition.

"That wasn't fair!" she protested, but Reggie laughed
and said: "You haven't heard any of his poetry. Listen to
this—

> And Jacob made for his wee Josie,
> A tartan coat to keep him cosie,
> And what for no?
> There was nae harm,
> Tae keep the lad baith safe and warm."

She laughed then too.

"Well, he had a good Scots tongue in his head. There's
nothing wrong with that."

They were going to have such a wonderful life together.
He had been going to teach her so much. They were going
to love each other so passionately and for so long.

She ached for him now. She tried to suck his spirit
from the air around her. But it was flesh and blood and
reality she needed. She hurried away from the university
again and caught a tramcar into town.

It was beginning to get dark. The city was ringed with
bonfires and a ceiling of sparks glistened all the time in
the air. Around the bonfires children and adults danced.
In every street there were rings of dancers. People had
been celebrating all day. Public houses had been so busy
that they had run dry and closed two hours earlier than the
normal time. Revellers spilled out on to the streets.
Thousands converged from the suburbs to the centre of
Glasgow. People buzzed from buildings as if the place was
a city of hives.

Every vehicle that passed was a throng of riotously
happy figures clinging to running-boards and luggage-

racks. Crowds of uniformed men roamed the streets drinking out of bottles. The air cracked and quivered with flags. Bugles blew. Trumpets tooted. Men in shirtsleeves pranced about the streets playing wildly on accordions to dancing crowds. Kilted pipers swaggered along followed by strutting, laughing children.

Young people marched in battalions through the centre of the city and were joined by thousands of others to besiege George Square.

By the time Julie crushed and jostled her way towards the square it was a solid mass of completely abandoned, riotously happy people, many of whom were climbing up the statues and trying to bring cheer to stone faces by the offer of whisky.

Coloured lights were strung over all the trees surrounding the square and the City Chambers were floodlit.

The most outstanding feature of the square, however, was the noise. Julie's ears had never been subjected to such a continuous racket. It had reached such a peak of loudness it was impossible to distinguish separate sounds. Impossible to hear the sounds of singing and cheering, the sounds of bagpipes, whistles, kettledrums, mouth organs, rattles, squibs and rockets. At a range of no more than thirty yards it was even impossible to hear the rumbustious music of the Glasgow Police Pipe Band. The air stretched with just one high-pitched yell like a locomotive's whistle that never died away.

The square dragged Julie in. Noise engulfed her, confused her. Someone whirled her into a dance but there was no room to dance and she stumbled and bumped about and laughed until she was breathless. Someone else gave her a swig out of a whisky bottle and tipped the bottle high so that she gulped too much and choked and spluttered. She danced arm in arm with a long line of service-men and -women. Then she found herself in another dance, arms hugging the waist of a man in front while someone behind clutched at her.

The dancing swung drunkenly backwards and forwards, round and round. Again and again bottles of whisky and beer were passed about and shared.

There were civilians, and there were servicemen of all kinds but Julie could only see air-force blue uniforms. She clung to one eventually, refused to let go, closed her eyes, rubbed and pressed her face against the muscly arm.

Lips close to her ear sent words wandering through her alcoholic haze.

"I'd better take you home, beautiful. Tell me where you live."

"Gorbals Cross," she slurred without opening her eyes. "And don't you dare say anything about the Gorbals, do you hear? There's plenty of good, honest, kindly, clean-living, decent . . ."

"Sure . . . Sure!"

She felt as if he were using her as a battering ram to force a way through the crowds but she clung on tightly and every now and again she opened her eyes and saw the blue material close to her face and was comforted.

She moaned with pleasure. Soon they would be out of the square, over the bridge across the Clyde, into dear old Gorbals, home, and bed.

# Chapter Sixteen

Catriona was in town spending some of her clothing coupons on much needed socks for the children when she felt tired and went into a café in Argyle Street for a reviving cup of tea. It was while she was sipping tea at the back of the café that she saw Sammy Hunter come in and sit down at a table near the door.

The sight of his fiery hair and his pugnacious broken-nosed face, with its jutting brows and cleft chin, catapulted her back to the night of the air-raid more vividly and immediately than anything else could. Sammy had come to Dessie Street to sort out his wife's things after she had been killed in a previous raid. His wife Ruth had left their home in Springburn to work in the bakery and stay with Catriona while Sammy was imprisoned in Maryhill Barracks for being a conscientious objector. One night, unknown to anyone, Ruth had gone to the Ritzy Cinema with Alec Jackson and the place had got a direct hit. Ruth had been buried under the debris.

Sammy had been released from detention shortly afterwards. Then while he was at Dessie Street there had been the other raid.

Sammy had dandled wee Robert on his knee. Sammy had carried the baby downstairs to the bakehouse lobby, the crowded, floury, heat-hazy place of mouth-watering smells where everybody thought they were safe.

She could see them now, she could hear their voices shouting to make themselves heard above the other sounds; the hysterical wailing of sirens, the low menacing thrum of

133

planes, the crack-crack of guns so near that they made windows rattle, the distant crump-crump of bombs.

"Hallo, Nellie . . . Aye, Tam . . . Come on, Lexy . . . Isn't this damnable, Angus . . . There you are, Sandy . . . Hallo, Baldy, lad . . . Here we are again, Catriona . . . How are you, Sammy . . ."

All her good friends and neighbours.

They had been singing, she remembered, when Dessie Street collapsed. She and Sammy had been two of the very few survivors.

She kept seeing him with her baby in his arms. Then suddenly Sammy's eyes flashed up as if he had sensed her anguished stare. The sight of her brought him immediately striding towards her.

"Catriona! I never noticed you come in."

"I was here a while before you. I'm finished my tea. I was just about to leave when I noticed you."

"Have another cup. Stay and tell me how you're getting on."

She smiled and nodded and he settled opposite her.

"Is your husband back yet?"

"Yes. We're in a room and kitchen in Byres Road but we're about to move into a bigger place in Botanic Crescent."

"He's managed to get another business then?"

"Yes, on a very good site. Do you know Byres Road at all?"

"I know it's a busy shopping centre. He should do well there."

"Yes, I believe he will. And of course it's a much bigger shop and bakehouse than the one in Dessie Street."

"So life is treating you well."

Her lips tried to stretch into a smile of agreement but trembled and failed. She shrugged instead.

"And you? Have you married again, Sammy?"

"No, still a widower and still in the house in Springburn.

I think you knew I was with The Friends' Ambulance Service?"

"Yes. The Society of Friends—they were the ones who helped you, weren't they?"

"I've been around a bit with them, I can tell you. You know, it's amazing what they do. They're a hardy crowd. Even the old ladies I've met seem spunky. There's one I know, well over seventy and believe it or not she still goes hill-climbing with her husband. They're great ones for enjoying nature. People have the wrong idea about them, Catriona. So did I at one time. Like everyone else I thought they were some narrow, strait-laced sect who wore white collars and high black hats. Not a bit of it. They believe in living their religion, not preaching it. They really care about people without wanting any recognition or glory for what they do. But just you read some books about the history of the Society and about some of the Quakers of the past. For such a small number of people it's amazing the amount of reform they've achieved and influence they've had."

He suddenly grinned. "Of course don't get me wrong. They're not all angels. I'm a pretty lousy one for a start."

"You're a Quaker?"

"Is it such an incredible idea?"

"I can't imagine you joining anything."

Sammy's muscular face tightened when he laughed.

"It's a lot different from the Army, you know. The exact opposite in fact. There's a wonderful sense of individual freedom and equality. Of course, this can lead to difficulties and disorganisation at times. And, as I say, they're not all angels. There's good and bad among them just the same as anywhere else, and sometimes individuality can stretch into eccentricity. Sometimes some of them nearly drive me mad. Yet I love their eccentricities and their mix-ups. It doesn't matter to me what they do. It's what they're trying to do, what they're struggling to achieve that's important. I don't know why but I feel I belong with them and feel at home. But you're quite right, I haven't joined. That's another thing I like about them. Nobody tries to convert you or put the slightest pressure on you to become a member."

"Are you still doing ambulance work for them?"

"Now that the war's over I'm having to think of going back to my old job. Although, to be honest, I don't feel the same about working in an office any more."

"Isn't it marvellous that it's all over?"

"Yes, of course. But at the same time, I can't help feeling depressed, Catriona."

After a minute or two in which he ordered more tea for both of them, she said:

"Because of all the people killed and injured, you mean?"

"Haven't you read anything about Hiroshima and Nagasaki?"

Her face twisted in distress.

"Poor things! I was just saying that to Melvin the other day, but he maintains they had to drop the atomic bombs to stop the war."

"And create a better world. A world fit for heroes to live in. That's what they always say. Now they're trying to justify the dropping of atomic bombs."

"Melvin was reading a report the pilot made and it sounded so business-like and ordinary. It said things like, 'The trip out to the target was uneventful.' Apparently he was awarded the Distinguished Flying Medal immediately he got back."

"Oh, yes," Sammy said bitterly. "He would! And they needn't kid us the raid was a last-minute emergency they were forced into. One of their precious brigadier-generals has let it out that the exact date for the dropping of the first atomic bomb was set well over a year ago. Anyway Japan was beaten before the bombs. Her navy was finished. Her air force wasn't able to defend the country. The new US bases had made invasion possible and the Japanese

136

armies on the mainland couldn't stand up against Slim's men."

Catriona said, "I keep thinking of the children."

He shook his head.

"I saw some of the pictures. Children with the patterns of their clothes burned into their skins. Imagine—the bomb was dropped at 9.15 a.m. Japanese time. Typists were taking the covers off their typewriters ready to start work. Shop assistants were behind their counters and customers were wandering in. Housewives were drinking cups of tea and children in school were just beginning to chant their lessons. Then suddenly there was this blinding flash and the whole city and everything and everyone in it, including emergency facilities, were crushed and burned by the terrific pressure and heat. And for miles outside there was and still is horror and suffering. And not only that, future generations are going to suffer."

"I don't want to imagine it. I get too upset."

He sighed.

"I don't enjoy thinking about these things either. But surely someone's got to. If we don't end war now—and I mean for good this time—war's going to end us."

"I don't see what we can do. We're just two individuals."

"The world's made up of individuals. Although I must admit I haven't a great deal of faith in our generation. There hasn't been much protest about the bomb or anything else, has there? But maybe the next generation, maybe your children will be different. Maybe they'll think for themselves and have more of a social conscience."

Catriona could not help laughing.

"All they're doing at the moment is playing football, getting dirty, tearing their good clothes, and, I'm afraid . . ." she eyed him mischievously, ". . . fighting!"

Sammy smiled and looked down at his cup in the shy, awkward way he had sometimes.

"Oh, I did plenty of that kind of fighting when I was young. What age are the boys now?"

"Fergus is nearly thirteen and Andrew will be eight in October."

"I probably wouldn't recognise them."

They drank their tea in silence for a while, both thinking of the changes that passing time had wrought in their lives. Then Sammy said:

"Do you ever see Alec Jackson these days?" Catriona's gaze betrayed momentary panic. She wondered if he knew about Alec and herself and the one shameful lapse that had resulted in baby Robert. Not that she was ashamed of Robert. Her thoughts scurried to blot out the word shame as if somehow Robert might be hurt by it. In case somehow, somewhere he still existed and might feel that she did not want him or love him. She had always wanted him and loved him. And she always would.

"Catriona?" Sammy's deep-set eyes were studying her curiously.

"Oh, sorry. I was dreaming. What were you saying, Sammy?"

"Remember that insurance man we used to have in Springburn?"

"Oh yes—Alec."

"His mother lived in one of the MacNair houses, didn't she? Ruth used to speak about him in her letters."

"Oh!" She felt even more uncertain of her ground.

"I never see him in Springburn now," Sammy went on. "I used to bump into him quite often."

"Look, Sammy. I'm awful sorry but I really will have to rush. The children are still on holiday from school and they get into so much mischief when I'm away like this. It's time I was getting home and making their tea."

He rose too, his craggy face wistful.

"It was nice seeing you again, Catriona."

Smiling and edging away from him towards the door she said:

"You must come and visit us after we're properly settled in the new house."

"I would like to very much."

"I'll drop you a note."

"Don't forget."

She waved goodbye and escaped from the café. It had been good to see him again but she felt confused and disturbed.

So many things had been happening recently one on top of the other that she did not know how to cope any more: the negotiations about the house in Botanic Crescent and the cleaning of it in preparation for moving in and the new business. The form-filling for that had been incredible, not to mention problems about staffing.

Melvin had persuaded her father to give up the good day-shift job he had in Farmbank and come over to Byres Road to help out. But, as she kept telling Melvin:

"Daddy doesn't keep well. You can't expect him to travel back and forward from Farmbank indefinitely."

"He can do a day shift here," Melvin said. "I'll do nights."

Melvin had never been afraid of hard work and Catriona had always regarded him as a practical down-to-earth person. Now, she was having to rethink even these basic attitudes. Melvin was very full of grand ideas but seemed so often to lack the initiative to organise them or put them into practice.

He needed her to help make his dreams of grandeur come true. Although he would rather have died than admit it. He had to have all the glory and the more she did the more credit he took.

He was the one who raved on to everyone about how his shop was going to be the poshest, best-looking business in Glasgow. She was the one who planned the colour scheme, went to search for paint and carried it back to Byres Road. She was the one who struggled up and down ladders, painting the place every spare minute she had.

He boasted that one day everyone in Glasgow would seek out MacNair's Bakery to buy their specialities. But it was she who thought up new ideas for recipes. The whisky liqueur cake had been her idea. At first Melvin had scoffed and sneered and said it would never work out. But together they had experimented with ingredients until a delicious sweet moist whisky-tasting confection had been produced. Already people were coming from all over Glasgow to buy it. The only drawback was that the ingredients were scarce. Even Melvin's friend who owned the pub nearby could not supply him with enough to meet the demand.

"But wait! Just wait!" Melvin said excitedly. "Rationing and shortages won't last for ever and then this will go like a bomb!"

The word bomb reminded her of what Sammy had been talking about.

She was reminded too of the family album old Mr MacNair kept in his room. Faded brown prints of mothers and fathers, and grandmothers and grandfathers, in their babyhood, their youth, their prime, then old age.

The pages flicked them past as hastily as life itself. And in that flicker of time it seemed so senseless for people to inflict suffering on each other.

"Oh, God, for the sake of the children," she thought. "Please don't let there be any more wars."

# Chapter Seventeen

"Now behave yourself," Catriona hissed at the children. "Remember there's a minister living in the next house!" She eased open the back door as if there might be crocodiles outside waiting to snap at her.

"So what?" Fergus said.

"So you behave yourself, that's what."

Irritably she punched his shoulder and immediately became more tense and anxious at the sight of the cold fury in his eyes. He did not say anything else and both boys left the house quietly. She knew however that there would be reprisals. Fergus would torment Andrew, perhaps by some constantly repeated act like knocking down Andrew's carefully set-up soldiers or perhaps just by following Andrew around peering closely at him all the time like a hypnotist.

Andrew would lose his temper and erupt in violence. Then Fergus would either hold the freckly-faced, wildly punching, struggling child at arm's length and taunt him with laughter, or he would twist his arms or hurt him in some other way.

She wondered if tormenting or bullying by older children happened in other families.

She realised that Fergus's tragic early years—losing his real mother and then being looked after by Lizzie next door in Dessie Street—must have something to do with his character. Lizzie had been a queer, twisted person who had tormented Fergus.

"I used to tell him I'd wait behind the door and pour

petrol over his daddy and set fire to him and burn him all up. I loved to see the expression on wee Fergie's face! What laughs I used to have!" Lizzie had told her.

It was not surprising that Fergus seemed twisted inside at times. Yet Catriona blamed Melvin too. He had constantly repressed the child's emotions in the mistaken belief that he was training him to be "the best-behaved boy in Glasgow".

In front of Melvin, Fergus made sure he was immaculately well behaved, was seen but not heard, never complained, never argued, never asked for anything, never cried, was never caught doing anything at all.

It took quick reflexes to catch even the change from the blue-eyed stare to the shifty gleam that meant a lie successfully told or something brewing that he thought he was going to get away with.

While Melvin had been in the Army the problem of Fergus had simmered down. She had tried to pay him a lot of attention, to listen patiently to his exaggerated tales about school and football and fights and his frightening gory war stories of air-raid victims or battle casualties he had heard or read about. Her own repressed, yet excitable nature, was irritated and distressed by his but she had all the time struggled with herself and tried to keep her voice floating along in pleasant normality.

"Gosh!" she'd say. "Fancy that, son. Oh, my goodness. Yes . . . fancy . . . oh, dear . . . What a shame . . . You don't say . . . Gosh!"

She felt it must be good for him to be able to express his emotions and if he was angry she did not discourage him from showing it and she tried to explain that if he was upset there was nothing wrong in finding release in tears.

No matter what he did to upset her she never remained angry for long. She forgave quickly and always made a point of tucking him in last thing at night with a goodnight smile and kiss.

She had been rewarded every now and again by unexpected bursts of affection, bear hugs that nearly strangled her and from which she was forced to seek escape. Or if she happened to have a cold or something wrong with her he would insist with demonic determination on looking after her.

"Don't get up, Mum. Don't get up. Just lie there. Lie there. I'll look after you."

"But I must get up, Fergus," she'd protest. "I've a hundred and one things to do."

He kept knocking her roughly back and holding her down.

"No. No! Don't get up, Mum. Don't get up. Just lie there. Lie there. I'll look after you."

She always lay for as long as she could, her eyes and ears closed against chaos in an effort to ignore dishes being broken and milk and sugar being spilled in Fergus's excitement in making her a cup of tea.

She considered her efforts well worth while but effort took energy and since Melvin had returned her energies were being stretched far beyond their normal limits.

There was so much to think about and do in connection with the shop. The old man had regained some enthusiasm and pride in acquiring a business again but he was too old to be of much practical help and just shuffled about the place getting in everyone's way.

Sometimes he did not bother going into the shop at all, and Melvin told him:

"Da, you might as well give up. Go on, retire and enjoy yourself!"

The only thing for which old Duncan never lost any talent was hanging on to money. It was like squeezing a lemon to get him to lay out capital.

Melvin wanted the bakehouse at the back of the shop to be the best and most modernly equipped in Glasgow.

But the old man kept repeating in his high-pitched nasal whine, "What was good enough for me is good enough for you. You've always had too many big ideas. That's always been your trouble!"

143

Melvin blustered on at his father in hearty good-natured attempts to keep things moving. He seldom allowed himself to become angry with the old man. This was a luxury he kept for Catriona. He nagged at her continuously, only stopping if someone else was there. He became a Jekyll and Hyde character with, for the most part, a surprisingly mild, amiable front to outsiders that only changed to a perverse whittling edge when he was alone with her.

It did not seem to matter what she did or how hard she worked, it was impossible to please him. He found something to criticise in everything she accomplished and yet he continued to pile on tasks big and small.

"You phone about that order, Catriona," he would say. "Tell them we've waited long enough for it. Tell them the war's over now. Tell them we don't need to put up with this and we're not going to!"

Then while she was phoning Melvin would keep whispering instructions, and afterwards he would grumble bitterly.

"You should have spoken up, been firmer. You sounded like a nervous schoolkid. What good do you think that's going to do? You're no use. You're weak, that's your trouble."

She tried to be firm and capable, to acquire a more forceful voice and brisker, more efficient manner, but it never seemed to do any good. Things got worse instead of better. Blame continued to be heaped on her head. His criticism lashed her already deeply rooted sense of guilt until to do something right became a masochist challenge. Her determination became desperation. She would do something right if it killed her.

Since they had moved into the house in Botanic Crescent exhaustion seemed to be already nibbling her life away. Half the time she wandered about in a daze. The mess the children made with their dirty feet or their untidiness, and her father-in-law with his tobacco all over the chairs and

144

carpets and his whisky and beer splashes, often reduced her to helpless weeping, not so much because she cared about these things, it was the measure of nagging she would have to suffer from Melvin if he saw the mess that tormented her.

Her mother came over to help wash the windows and scrub what seemed miles of floors and stairs, yet she only made things worse and tightened the screws of her secret anxieties.

"May the Good Lord have mercy on you, Catriona. That man's trying to kill you like he killed his first wife!"

"I'm perfectly all right," she assured her mother, but cries echoed louder and louder inside her from a deep well of fear.

"May God forgive you, Catriona. You know perfectly well that's a downright lie. I don't know what he did to his first wife but I've seen some of the things that man has done to you. Remember how he forced you to go to the Empire Exhibition and you nearly gave birth in the middle of all these thousands of folk? It was disgusting as well as dangerous. Then there was that horrible miscarriage you had . . ."

She kept on scrubbing the floors and her mother kept on talking.

"He's trying to work you to death, that's what he's trying to do, sacrifice you to his own conceit. I told you no good would come of you marrying that man. I told you you would be punished. You should leave now before it's too late. Think of the children. Do you want them to be left alone in this big house with that man?"

Catriona wanted to leave. But it was all very well to talk blithely about leaving. It reminded her of Melvin's big talk and how she was always left to face and work out the small humdrum practicalities of the matter.

It was all very well too for a decision like this to be made and put into practice by someone happily free from the exhausting effects of the situation; someone whose health was not affected, someone who was fresh in mind and body; someone who was not debilitated by neurotic pressures from childhood. Someone with a different character.

Directly she moved out of Melvin's house her mother would leap on her like a man-eating tiger. If she escaped from Melvin how could she escape from her mother? What could she do without money? Where could she go? Accommodation of any kind was at a premium. Squatters were moving into flats, houses, even offices, shops and Nissen huts. What could she take with her? Melvin would certainly allow her nothing, not one teaspoon, not one face towel, not even a suitcase. He had always made it very clear that his money had supplied everything and everything was his.

She would have to leave without telling him and when he was out so that she could scramble a few necessities together and dart furtively away clutching the children and cases and cardboard boxes. But Melvin worked nights and was in the house most of every day. He slept badly if he slept at all and the slightest movement wakened him. How could she leave without him knowing, when at all odd unexpected times he was liable to appear at her elbow with blood-orange eyes and moustache spiking over sour mouth?

Over and over again she tried to plan how she could organise the practical details of escape and how she could overcome all the difficulties. Threads of action kept spinning across her mind, weaving this way and that in a web which strangled her with its complexity.

And all the time her mother nagged at her about Melvin and Melvin nagged at her about her mother.

"She's an absolute menace, that woman. You keep her out of my house, do you hear?"

But he no longer said anything to her mother's face and this apparent sign of weakness gave more persistence to her mother's voice. She felt like a bone between two dogs, a thing to be used or misused.

Then Da began to worry her by doing dangerous things like dropping burning paper or matches on the floor of his room. Singed, smoking, smelling patches and holes multiplied on the carpet and she began to notice burns on his sheets and blankets too. She realised his hands were getting shaky with age but the knowledge only increased her fears that one night he would set the house on fire and burn the children in their beds.

She worried constantly about the children yet her irritation with them seemed to increase with her concern. Their bickering if she asked for their help became unbearable. It was one thing Fergus ministering to her. It was quite another matter if she asked him to tidy up his room or weed the back garden. She always told Andrew to do his share but in a few minutes the bickering would start.

"You left these there!" Fergus accused.

"I did not!" Andrew protested.

"Come on, Fatso, put them away."

"No! I hate you. Big Skinnymalink!"

"What did you say? What did you say?"

Then there would be a yelp or howl or scream of pain from Andrew and she would rush through to slap wildly at Fergus or at Fergus and Andrew and cry out near to tears.

"Oh, get out, get out of my sight, both of you. I'll do it myself."

Yet there was an affection between the boys too. If someone else attacked Andrew and the opponent was too big for Andrew to tackle successfully by himself, he would shout:

"I'll get my big brother to you."

Fergus always battled to his aid.

More and more each day she seemed to split in two. One part of her knew the right thing to do, the other tormented herself by doing the opposite. Her mind pointed out with painful clarity that she should not have snapped at Andrew:

"Oh, shut up and get out of my way. Why can't you just

leave me alone? It's Mummy, Mummy, Mummy, all the time. I never get a minute's peace."

He had been telling her something of importance that had happened at school.

She should not have shouted at Fergus:

"No, you cannot go out to play. You should be working, not playing. Why should a big useless article like you do nothing but play while I'm being worked into the ground!"

There was no reason for him to stay in and nothing he could do at that particular moment.

It was Melvin and the old man she really felt like shouting at. But she was afraid of Melvin because he seemed to be waiting for any excuse to start nagging at her. His voice had become like rat's teeth gnawing the very flesh from her bones. She found it safest to say as little as possible to Melvin. No use being angry with Da either. He was getting more and more fuddled.

Often she started quite sensible conversations with him and then for no apparent reason he would become "thrawn" and contradict something about which they had previously been agreeing. Then the conversation would rapidly deteriorate into a maze of contradictions and foolishness.

She knew she was taking it out on the children and was tortured with regret yet she continued to surprise them with sudden vicious outbursts that sometimes reduced them both to tears. Sometimes she wept helplessly along with them. Then in an effort to console them and to sooth the pain of her conscience she gave them money and coupons with which to buy sweets or to pay for a visit to the local cinema.

If Melvin happened to be there, however, she did not get the chance to console the children. He immediately pounced on her in front of them and verbally tore her to shreds.

"You're weak," he kept saying. "You're no use."

Every despicable fault imaginable was attributed to her. It was like stripping her naked before the children's eyes and she hated him for it. She found herself retreating in an ever-shrinking pattern of behaviour and speech in order to avoid any confrontation with Melvin. Fergus soon realised this and became completely undisciplined behind his father's back knowing that she dare not say anything to him or call on Melvin's help. A kind of blackmail situation arose. If Fergus did not get what he wanted or was not allowed to do as he liked, he would either complain to Melvin, or make Andrew suffer, and Andrew never dared tell what happened to him no matter how much she questioned him about why he was crying in bed at night, or why he was terrified to go upstairs alone. Occasionally she would find out through Madge's children that Fergus had said there were ghosts under Andrew's bed and a witch hiding behind the door in the bathroom.

Or something precious to someone in the house would disappear or be mysteriously broken.

Melvin always blamed her and displayed his anger by haranguing her with words and upsetting her in whatever way came into his mind. Once he had grabbed her best dress from the wardrobe and torn it to shreds literally under her nose. Often he turned Andrew's photograph face to the wall or he would make a fool of the child, until Andrew complained that it was obviously better to be a bad boy. He shouted at her angrily, his freckles like brown chocolate drops against a white milky skin.

"Fergus does what he likes and nobody says a word to him. But everybody gets on to me. It's not fair. I'm just getting fed up with it!"

He stamped away, desperate to hide from her his tears of rage and frustration.

She heard afterwards, again from one of Madge's children, that Andrew had made an attempt at running away from home but after a few hours he returned because he felt hungry.

Visions of Andrew wandering about lost in the dark tormented her. Catriona tried to protect him, cushion him from further upsets. She always kept alert, keyed up, listening, watching, trying to keep track of where everybody was all the time and if Andrew was alone in a room with either Fergus or Melvin she kept making excuses to be there too. Even if she were in the middle of making a meal and Andrew was in the sitting-room she would keep coming through to make casual conversation with Melvin or to pretend she was looking for something.

Sometimes she told herself that if she could just hang on long enough things would get better. Fergus was a good boy at heart and he would surely grow out of this difficult stage. Melvin was worried because he had used up all his money paying for the house and furnishing it and it was a terrible strain on him to be continuously fighting to prise money out of the old man in order to get the business properly organised. What he had suffered during the war, of course, could account for much of his irrational behaviour. Often she would look at Melvin's ravaged face and know she could not leave him. Yet she felt just as certain she could not go on the way she was doing.

# Chapter Eighteen

Catriona began to suffer from headaches, and coughs, and pains in her chest, and legs, and back, and stomach, and throat. Often she vomited. In attempts to relieve her perplexing symptoms she experimented with different tablets and powders and pills. She had become so convinced that there was no solution to her problems and that no one could help her, it even seemed hopeless to go to a doctor. She suspected that anxiety and unhappiness lay at the the root of her symptoms and she could not see how a bottle of medicine would be able to cure that.

"Snap out of it!" Melvin kept saying. "Pull yourself together!"

It was no good. She did not know how to pull herself together and eventually she decided to try going to the local doctor.

He was an elderly man with a grey woolly moustache like Melvin's, a stooping posture, a non-existent neck and a continuous little grin as if many years ago his mouth had cramped in that position. He shook hands when she shyly entered the room in his house that he used as a surgery. He shook hands most politely when he ushered her out again a few minutes later. He had not even bothered to examine her.

He had scribbled a prescription, grinned and assured her that everything was "just nerves".

The tablets made her feel dopey and depressed and when Melvin found out she had been to the doctor he behaved like a madman.

"You disgust me," he spat. "I could never feel anything for you any more."

She felt as if she were going mad herself. Somehow she could not accustom herself to Melvin's illogical behaviour.

"I don't understand," she said. "What have I done now?"

"Don't act innocent with me. I know your sly filthy mind."

"Are you talking about my visit to the doctor?"

"It didn't matter to you that you were my wife."

"What has being your wife got to do with it?"

"That's typical! It doesn't matter that you're my wife. You'd let any Tom, Dick or Harry muck about with you."

"I only went to the doctor because I felt ill."

"What do you mean—ill? Don't give me that. What's wrong with you, then? Tell me! Come on. Tell me. Is there anything wrong with your lungs? Or your stomach? Or your heart? Come on! Come on! Tell me!"

The bulbous eyes staring out wildly from dark sunken rings frightened her. His voice stirred up fear too. It was a vulture's claw intent on destroying her.

He is mad, she thought. And for some reason or for no reason he is trying to make me the same; it sounds melodramatic and no one will ever believe me, but it's true. The terrible isolation of her predicament and her inability to cope with it terrified her.

She tried to push him aside and go into another room but he followed close behind.

"What's wrong, then? Tell me! Is there something wrong with your heart?"

She wondered what anyone would say if they saw him now, the crazy red eyes, the wildly quivering cheeks.

"No."

"He massaged it for you, did he?"

"Get away from me! Leave me alone!"

She ran into the hall and he darted after her. She hurried up the stars sucking in little gasping, panicky breaths but all the time silently pleading with herself to keep calm.

*Keep calm and you'll be all right. He's trying to break you, make you scream with hysteria. Just ignore him. Keep calm and you'll be all right!*

She fought her way from one room to another, pushing, punching, clawing at him, struggling desperately to close each door between them. But he always proved stronger and heaved it in and his voice although he never raised it, became more and more obscene. The only way she could escape from him was to run outside. There she walked the streets worrying about the children and trying to gather enough courage to return.

Eventually she could not stand it any longer. Her nerves strained far beyond caring about money or accommodation or anything, she waited until Melvin left for work one night and then hurriedly began flinging clothes into a case.

"Why are you doing that?" Fergus's pale eyes watched her curiously.

"Don't just stand there!" she cried. "Quick! Get a box or a message bag or something and stuff in everything you want to take. Tell Andrew to do the same. We're going back to stay at Granny's for a while."

Out in the dark cold street, hurrying penguin-like, stiff-armed with heavy cases and parcels tucked underneath, she was palpitating, sweating, choking with terror in case Melvin should suddenly materialise out of the fog and confront her.

Now even her mother's home in Farmbank seemed a haven of peace and safety in her mind. She had staggered the length of Great Western Road with the boys hurrying and complaining behind her when a tap on her shoulder made her jump and brought a high-pitched strangled sound to her throat like the squeal of a trapped animal.

Both Fergus and Andrew giggled at her unexpected reaction and Fergus said:

"I only wanted to ask if we were going to see Dad in the bakehouse first."

Shivering, huge-eyed with hatred, she whirled on them.

She even hated Andrew for laughing at her and not understanding how terrified and ill she felt.

"No, we're not. Stop that idiotic snickering, both of you! Get in front of me so that I can see what you're doing and hurry up or we'll never get to Farmbank tonight."

Never before had Glasgow seemed so enormous, or so teeming with strangers, prosperous, successful strangers of good character with orderly lives and respectable homes to go to. Struggling along the road with the cases bumping against and wobbling her legs and the parcels under her arms beginning to come undone she felt ashamed, a failure, an inadequate, an embarrassment, someone who did not fit in, who was no more than a piece of flotsam blown along the street by the wind.

The journey to her mother and father's house was one of the worst in her life. She had no clear recollection how she eventually got there.

There was only the relief of the door opening and the lighted lobby sucking her in. The babble of voices, her mother's, her father's, Fergus's, Andrew's. Then a hot cup of tea being forced into her hands.

"That man won't dare come here. And if he does he'll have me to reckon with," her mother assured her. "Don't worry, Catriona, you're safe here!"

But even on the sofa crouched behind the bars of the chairs she did not feel safe. Nor did she feel at home.

An urgent obsessive need to defend herself had become all powerful. Alerted by this into a continuous high pitch of tension she could not, dare not, sleep.

Rootless, isolated, she listened to sounds lapping far away outside her. The boys giggling and bouncing on the bed-settee next door, her father's mock growl as he chastised them, only to make the giggles and the squeals swell louder and louder. The strong monotonous thump-thump of her mother's feet as she strode busily, happily about.

"Now, now, come on, boys, that's enough nonsense! Finish your piece on jam and say your prayers. Granny and

Grandpa are going to bed. Come on, Robert, get through to the bedroom and leave them alone. You're worse than they are."

"Our Father which art in heaven . . ."

"Fergus, don't you dare carry on like that while you're saying your prayers. Do you want God to strike you down dead for making a fool of him? Clasp your hands and close your eyes. Now both together."

"Our Father which art in heaven . . ."

Chanting voices balancing along the edge of hysterical laughter.

Doors shutting. Giggles muffled by blankets. Long black silence.

Sleep stealing across. Then jerkily deserting her.

Dusty grey light. A mosquito net through which shabby furniture looms over her. Everything was too big and too close in the overcrowded room, including her mother now up and dressed and pinning an old felt hat on top of her thick coiled hair.

"I'm going along to see if I can get anything for you and the children's breakfast. They might have some dried egg and I could whip up a nice omelette. I looked in your bag, by the way, and found your ration books. I won't be long. You get up and set the table and put the kettle on. Your daddy's away to work but I haven't wakened the boys yet."

She went away humming cheerfully to herself but she had only been gone five or ten minutes and Catriona was struggling, shivering into her clothes when the letter-box clanged impatiently.

Secretly cursing her mother for the headache the noise had triggered off she hurried to open the door and was caught off guard to find Melvin.

The sight of his broad-shouldered figure, his bushy moustache, his bulbous eyes, his twitching face filled her with undiluted hatred.

Pushing past her he said:

"What's the meaning of this?"

For a moment she was tempted to run from the house instead of following him back into the living-room but she had no shoes or stockings on.

"I left a note."

"What do you mean—you left a note?" He pulled out a piece of paper and stared incredulously at it. "'Melvin, I'm leaving you'!"

"There wasn't any use saying anything else."

"What do you mean, there wasn't any use saying anything else?"

Sheer animal self-preservation made her wish he were dead. A basic need to defend herself, to survive at all costs, took overriding possession of her. Eyes normally guileless pools of amber, narrowed to yellow slivers of malevolence and suspicion. Soft vulnerable mouth hardened and twisted and became ugly.

"Aw, shut up!" she flung at him and snatched up her stockings and turned her back on him as she tugged them on.

"What do you mean—shut up?"

"Go away! Die! Disappear!"

"Oh, charming! You're a great wife, you are! Supposed to be a goody-goody Christian as well."

"I don't want to be anything to you. Just go away, Melvin, and forget you ever saw me. That's all I ask. Just leave me in peace. I don't want to have anything more to do with you."

"Don't talk rubbish. You're my wife. Get your coat on. We're going home right now."

"No!"

"What do you mean—no?"

"Goodbye, Melvin."

"What do you mean—goodbye?"

"I've a thumping headache."

"Well, hurry up then. Get your coat on and come on home. I can't stand here all day. I've been slaving my guts out in the bakehouse while you've been here snoring and enjoying yourself."

"You'd better go before my mother gets back."

"Is this the case you took? I'll pack it. You get your coat on."

"Are you deaf or stupid or something?"

Immediately he tucked clothes into the case she swooped on them and scattered them wildly over the floor. Words tumbled recklessly from her mouth.

"I don't want to have anything to do with you. I hate you. I loathe you. I despise the very sight of you. Can I make it any clearer than that? Get out! Get out of here before I get my mother to fetch the police."

He suspended in uncertainty for a minute. Then he began to shake like an old man. He looked like his father.

"You don't know what you're saying."

"It's finished, that's what I'm saying."

His face twisted, screwing out tears. His voice howled up an octave.

"You can't leave me. Not after all I've suffered for you and worked for you all these years. If you leave me I'll have suffered and worked all these years for nothing."

The hatred for the chains of guilt he was welding came straight from hell.

"I wish you were dead!"

He was blubbering now and moaning.

"I will be dead if you leave me. I'll commit suicide. I'll kill myself." He stretched out hands, doughy brown floury hands with black treacle hardening under square nails. "Catriona!"

"Don't touch me!"

"I'll kill myself." He began banging his head against the wall. "I'll kill myself. I'll kill myself!"

"You've wakened the children!"

She could hear their half-awake, half-frightened voices growing louder and keener with apprehension.

"Mummy, where are you? What's wrong? Mummy!"

Hatred built up like steam pressure in her head. She wanted to pounce on Melvin like a wild animal, strangle him, exterminate him, rid herself of him once and for all. Then, suddenly, the violence of her emotions exhausted her. Words dragged out heavily:

"I don't care what you do, Melvin. I don't care about anything."

Right away Melvin brightened.

"It's all right, boys," he shouted, mopping his face with a big greasy handkerchief. Then after noisily trumpeting into it he began issuing instructions to her.

"Tell them to come on later. Tell them to explain to your mother about me coming for you. Tell them . . ."

She made her way through to the sitting-room, ignoring the rest of what he was saying. Then having seen to the children she allowed Melvin to hustle her from the house.

She longed for help. For days afterwards she thought continuously of her two friends Julie and Madge. Julie had disappeared without a word. Mrs Vincent had called to enquire about her. It was from Mrs Vincent she learned that Julie had left her job at Morton's. The manageress at Morton's had told Mrs Vincent Julie had gone away to live and work in England.

Madge was no longer in Huntley Gardens. Apparently the police and the owner's men had broken into the house and moved Madge's furniture out on to the street and when she tried to stop them they had manhandled her and Alec had lost his head and set about them with his fists. He had been arrested and was serving a sentence in prison.

Madge and the children were in Barnhill. She had gone twice to the institution to see Madge but on both occasions Madge and the children were out. Apparently they were put out every morning and had to stay out all day. It was only at night they were given a roof over their heads.

If it had not been for Melvin she would have had

Madge living with her in Botanic Crescent. Despite the obvious harassment of adding the noise and problems of seven children to her own two, it would have been a comfort to have her friend beside her.

Melvin had nearly burst a blood vessel at the mere idea. Completely recovered from his weeping fit he raged on at her. She had never really had any hope of him agreeing to give shelter to Madge and the children and she had not nearly enough energy left to fight him.

She wept in secret for her friend. It was dreadful to think of a woman, any woman, losing all her possessions, her security, her home, being unable to protect her children.

She knew only too well what it was like.

Like a monster for ever crouched in some secret corner, the night of the air-raid towered up and spilled long shadows of horror across her mind. Recent glimpses of other insecurities added to her distress. She felt again the rootlessness and the shame of walking the streets with nowhere to go.

She cupped her hands across her mouth and nursed herself.

Now Melvin had made a will. He had told her quite casually, making no secret of the fact that he had left the new house to Fergus.

"You're no flesh and blood of mine, you see," he had explained to her in front of the child. "Fergus is my son!"

It was like the air-raid happening all over again every time she thought of it. It was as if she were already dispossessed like Madge, homeless, without any rights or place.

All her life, as far back as she could remember, she had longed for security, had played houses by herself as a child and pretended she had one. Continuously, day and night it had been her dream.

She realised now that it was a basic need for every woman and it did not matter about the size of the place or what it looked like. It was the feeling of having it that mattered, of belonging, of having roots, of being safe.

Once again the world caved in, dust parched her throat. Things loved disintegrated, were temporary, unreal, like everything else.

And she was frightened.

# Chapter Nineteen

Julie moaned and retched violently over the kitchen sink. The brown paper blind was drawn down in case someone from outside might see and it enclosed the room in a funereal stillness.

Her skin clung like wet ice and prickled with pins and needles. She willed herself not to faint.

She kept remembering how when she was sick as a child one of her mother's hands supported her brow, the other hand cuddled tightly round her shoulders. She remembered a cotton apron, a soft body and a strong voice.

*You're all right, hen. Mammy's here. You're Mammy's brave wee lassie.*

She had been thinking about Mammy a lot recently. She used to clamber into the kitchen bed beside her when Dad was on nightshift and Mammy would sing her to sleep, often with a proper song or rhyme but sometimes with just a few repetitive words, lilting softly.

> *Mammy's bonnie wee lassie,*
> *Mammy's bonnie wee lass.*

The sickness died down and she forced herself to wash her face at the cold water tap. Then she brushed her hair and slashed on fresh lipstick. She spent most of the time alone in the house but she was determined that she would keep herself looking decent. Her father had never been one to stay indoors and now, because he felt helpless and did not know what to do, he kept well out of her way.

Despite all her efforts, however, her hair lost its bounce, her face pinched in.

Her morning sickness was supposed to go away after the first few months but nearly nine months had passed now and she was still plagued with it; sometimes it lasted, off and on, for most of the day. It only needed her dad to hawk or give one of his phlegmy coughs to set her rushing boking to the sink.

As soon as she had discovered she was pregnant she stopped working in Morton's and told a story about going down to live in England. Her first thought was of the disgrace. Shame hardened around her, locked her into herself. She vowed that if anyone said anything she would spit in their eye and tell them to go to hell. She froze out her father, her glittering eyes warning him not to mention her pregnancy, daring him to utter one word.

A job in a small general store in one of the back streets of Gorbals helped her financially until her condition became too obvious. Then she left and shut herself up in the house and told her father he must do all the shopping. She would not put her foot outside the door except to go to the lavatory and she suffered agonies trying to avoid that because the lavatory was outside on the stair. She always listened just to make sure the stair was quiet before hurrying out.

Her father tried his best but often lost the shopping list she gave him and did not remember all the messages and sometimes, despite her angry warnings that she was not coming to the door for anyone, he forgot his key.

At first she whiled away the long hours by busying herself scrubbing and polishing and cleaning out cupboards until every inch of the place sparkled and she could have defied anyone to find a speck of dust or even the faintest smudge of a fingermark anywhere.

Then she got so fat and heavy and ungainly she could not manage the cleaning. She still kept the house as best she could but it was a difficult and breathless task to reach up or bend over or kneel down and once down it was a terrible struggle to get back up.

Food acquired an urgency, became intensely important, something to drool over and dream about and look forward to. If her father forgot to bring the sweets or biscuits she had been craving for, disappointment was so keen she sometimes shamed herself by bursting into heartbroken tears.

Proud and bitterly ashamed, hard and resilient, yet with an aura of vulnerability about her, she wandered through the house like a bewildered child.

Her only contact with outside, apart from her father, was the papers and from them she soaked up a miscellany of news. She read copies of the *Glasgow Bulletin* avidly, hoarded them, re-read old ones. She fastened especially on serious items in an effort to exercise her mind and keep herself from stagnating as each long, blank hour followed another.

"It is an accepted fact that war is accompanied by a lowering of the standard of morals and conduct. Within the lifetime of a generation it has been possible to observe the effect of two wars upon delinquency and crime and if the results have been very much as one would expect they are not the less deplorable on that account . . . . . . The culminative effect of six years of war has been to weaken the moral fibre and the powers of resistance. The stages of dissolution through which Britain has passed are familiar and need not be recapitulated but the black-out, the break-up of homes, the destruction of property by bombing, rationing and the black market have all left their marks upon the civilian population.

Since each war is more barbarous than the last and since the 1939–1945 conflict was fought with an unparalleled savagery and at closer quarters than its predecessor it follows that life has never been held so cheap as it is today.

The picture of early post-war Britain which has its

counterpart in the United States is unlovely. London has its crime wave which ranges from highly organised theft to kidnapping and worse. Glasgow has been shocked by a particularly brutal murder and everywhere crime is on the increase ...''

Now she flung the papers aside. War ... war ... It was enough to make anybody sick.

Mammy used to say, "I'm glad you're not a boy, hen. They just take boys away and use them as cannon fodder."

She took an unexpected pain in her abdomen but it eased away after a couple of minutes. She blamed it on all the retching she had been doing and a strained muscle was the last thing she wanted with her date only about a couple of weeks away. She did not know much about birth but she imagined that strong abdominal muscles would be a better help than weak ones.

Impulsively she hauled herself up from the kitchen chair and trailed through to the room to search in one of the drawers for a photo of Mammy. Then, finding one, she stood staring at it for a long time.

Mammy's health had broken eventually. Probably having a late baby and then losing the wee boy did not help.

She had been slightly taller than Dad, a fine-looking woman with a proud lift to her head, a gleam of courage in her eyes and a touch of red in the brown hair pulled severely back and plaited.

The photograph of Mammy was in her hands when the knocking at the door jerked her attention irritably away and made her slip it into the pocket of her smock.

She had a good mind to ignore the knocking and keep her father out. She had threatened him more than once to do it. Pain niggled her again and she leaned against the sideboard for a minute or two before forcing herself to go and open the door just a crack so that she could see but not be seen.

Mrs Vincent was standing on the doormat as small and

slim and expensive-looking as ever. Normally her perfume was something Julie envied. Now it brought nausea to trigger off another bout of sickness.

"Julie! I knew you hadn't gone away. I just knew it! Oh, my dear, your face! You look so pale and ill!"

Julie turned away in anguish, fighting for dignity, but jerky spasms persisted in heaving her body and she had to run to the sink.

Afterwards she splashed cold water on her face and brushed her hair before looking round at Mrs Vincent who had followed her into the kitchen.

She saw the older woman's horror, saw the minister's daughter shrinking from the evil, fallen woman, saw Mrs Vincent's struggle with herself, her expressions changing like butterflies fluttering backwards and forwards across her face.

At last her loyalty to Reggie won. She took a little breath like a sigh then said:

"I'll do all I can to help you. What do you need? A new smock? A nightdress? Baby clothes?"

Before she sat down her gloved hand lightly brushed the fireside chair clean.

"I don't need any help, thank you," Julie replied. "I've knitted one set of baby clothes. I won't need any more. I'm having it adopted."

There was a tiny silence then Mrs Vincent said:

"Yes, of course. That's very sensible of you. And after it's all over, don't you think you would be better to come and stay with me? That's what Reggie would have wanted."

"I have a good home here. Thanks all the same."

"Oh, dear, I do feel guilty. Reggie did tell me to look after you. I'm sure if you had been over in Kelvinside with me this . . ." Her face creased as if she were in pain and she forced her eyes just for a moment to rest on Julie's swollen belly. ". . . This terrible thing would never have happened."

Julie reached for her cigarettes, lit one and tossed the match into the fire with a careless defiant gesture.

"What has happened has nothing to do with you. But if you must know, I love this man even more than I loved Reggie. He's crazy about me too. But he's married." She shrugged. "That's my hard luck. We love each other, that's the main thing, and I've known him for some time. He didn't pick me up off the street, you know!"

Mrs Vincent's face tightened again but she said:

"I would still like to help. Are you going into hospital?"

"Yes." Energetically Julie puffed at her cigarette. "Ten days from now."

"Are you sure you have everything you need? A confinement is so expensive. Have you something really pretty to wear in bed? It makes such a difference to how one feels. I always believe in having a really pretty nightdress and négligée."

"Yes. I can imagine. I've still got the one from my honeymoon. It'll do."

"I'll get you something else. And some of the other little things that make such a difference. A nice talcum, a good soap."

"You've no need. Thanks all the same." She turned away, her breath catching with another pain. "I'll make you a cup of tea. The kettle's on the boil."

The thought occurred to her that she might have started labour. Doctors could make mistakes. Or something might have gone wrong.

Mrs Vincent peeled off her gloves and smoothed them neatly across her lap.

"Thank you, my dear. That would be nice. I've been worrying about you so much and then finding you like this . . . I've developed quite a migraine. Nervous tension, do you think?"

"You should go home and lie down. But drink up your tea first."

Mrs Vincent gave a little sighing breath.

"Think about coming to stay with me, Julie. It would be so nice to have you. I get lonely at times. After this is all over we'll talk about it again, shall we?"

"I belong here."

"You would soon settle in and there's your friend in the crescent now—young Mrs MacNair."

Stiff-faced, Julie watched her taking her time over her tea. Sipping it slowly, delicately, then each time replacing the cup gently, quietly.

"I thought she looked a bit peaky the last time I saw her," Mrs Vincent murmured between sips. "Of course, I don't think she has any domestic help and those houses are rather large. Then I believe she pops in quite often to the shop. I hear the business is doing very well."

At last she rose. "Tomorrow I'll go into town and buy you some nice little odds and ends. No, you can't dissuade me, my dear. I can be very determined when I like."

Just before she left she leaned forward and pecked Julie on the cheek.

Julie closed the door and returned to the kitchen. She felt unexpectedly upset. The pain was distressing enough but now a new emotional upheaval suddenly gripped her chest and sent it lurching into big noisy breaths, like sobbing without tears, and made her plead to the empty room, "Mammy. Mammy."

The grinding pain intensified, became her only world, demanded all her attention. Then it died away again and she became aware of the sweat trickling down her face.

Long ago she had saved up enough for a taxi. The money was ready in her purse but her dad was supposed to phone for one and have it come to the close to collect her. Her case was ready packed. She had everything arranged.

Slowly she made her way through to the room and collected her case. It was an old scuffed one from Woolworth's and the cardboard it was made of showed through the brown paint. She struggled into her coat then went over to the window.

Her father was standing down at the corner and she fought to open the window and call out.

"Dad!"

He looked up in surprise. "Eh?"

"Phone, right away."

"My God! Aye, aw right, hen."

The journey back to the kitchen was excruciating. Her grip tightened on her case and, still clutching it close to her, she sat down to wait for the taxi. She would arrive in style. That's how she had planned it. Then with any luck everything would all be over by morning. Life would return to normal. She would be herself again as if nothing had happened.

# Chapter Twenty

If it had been an ex-Navy camp maybe Alec would have felt more at home but the Hughenden Playing Fields off Great Western Road, which belonged to the Hillhead High School, had been requisitioned by a Royal Air Force Balloon Squadron in 1939.

Now its Nissen huts sheltered a gypsy band of squatters, travelling people, rootless ones, displaced persons, the rubbish dirtying the skirts of respectable West End society, the flotsam washed up by war.

Most of the men were ex-servicemen. Some of them had had their wives and families in married quarters while they had been in the forces and after demob had been unable to find alternative accommodation. Others had returned to find that their homes had been destroyed by air-raids. Others like Alec had been unable to get work, could not pay their rent and been forced to quit.

He had been in several places, hanging on, trying to make the best of it until workmen came to cut off water and electricity and tear up floorboards and fling his furniture and belongings out on to the street.

He had missed death while serving in the Navy. Since the war he had died a thousand deaths.

The Nissen hut, as Madge said, was better than being in Barnhill but they had no privacy, especially from the children, and any amenities that existed were communal. Everybody in the camp went to the same place for ablutions and to wash their clothes as best they could in cold water. There were no facilities for ironing.

He did not mind the communal bit so much. He liked plenty of people around. What he did suffer from was the lack of clean, pressed clothes. He had always been a natty dresser and it was an acute humiliation to go about in a creased suit or wrinkled raincoat or grubby crumpled shirt. Embarrassment made his eyes become evasive and he acquired the habit of looking down as much as possible when he walked outside the camp with the ostrich-like hope that if he saw nothing, nobody would see him. If anyone, especially a woman, spoke to him he could still come out with some of the old patter and his eyes still twinkled at them, but with hasty sideways glances that betrayed a furtive restlessness. His walk did not lose its sailor's roll or its Glasgow swagger but the movements shrank, lost their jaunty bounce, became a gentle imitation.

Not that he walked much around the Great Western Road area. He did not like this part of Glasgow. He realised of course that his views were jaundiced by the unpleasant experiences he and his family had suffered in the West End.

He supposed it looked all right. Plenty of big houses and trees. Sometimes he went for a walk with Madge and the weans and looked at them all. Madge loved to stare at houses. She would keep crying out in admiration.

"Oh, Sadie, look at this one, hen. Look at its lovely big windows. How many rooms do you think this one'll have, eh?" Or, "Agnes, would you just look at that. Oh, my, isn't that lovely, hen?"

In the silent avenues, terraces, gardens and lanes where no children played, Madge's voice boomed out with excruciating loudness. Not that they needed Madge's voice to draw attention to themselves. The mere fact that there was nine of them crowding along the pavement was enough. In the camp they blended in with the others. In Springburn's busy streets they would have merged into the background too. Here, however, they were vulnerable as if a spotlight was aimed at them, ruthlessly picking out every shabby detail.

He became acutely conscious of his own seedy appearance, of Madge's down-at-heel shoes and dirty ankles, of the children's motley mixture of ill-fitting clothes, of skimpy coats, with dresses drooping underneath them, and of Hector and Willie's knobbly wrists protruding from their jackets.

Charlie looked worst of all. His mouth was plugged with a dummy-teat but his nose was usually running and his nappy drooped down at his ankles. His clothes never seemed to meet. Bare skin always showed in the middle. Often Charlie was left to stagger or crawl along on his own, getting dirtier and dirtier, until Alec lifted him and tried to wipe him with a handkerchief. He was fond of Charlie. The other children had grown away from him and now resented him as a symbol of authority.

Madge kept shouting at them.

"I'll tell your daddy on you, you rotten wee midden!" Or, "Daddy'll throttle you, I'm warning you." Or she would command him:

"Do something with these weans! Don't just loaf about like the useless big article you are!"

Coming back to the camp after one of their walks, he felt especially diminished, as if all the grand houses all around were only there to emphasise the fact that he was no use as a provider. All he could manage for his family was a dark corrugated iron cave.

He tried to blot out his thoughts in drink as much as he could and one night after he had had a few and Madge was nagging at him, he suddenly lost his head and struck her.

Looking back on it he sometimes thought she had been purposely egging him on. The way she had been acting anyone would have thought the war and everything else was his fault.

"Aye, you've always been all right, haven't you?" she sneered. "Sailing around the world, having your way with women every chance you could get. Talk about the proverbial Smart Alec. Well, you're not so smart now, are you, eh? An unemployed ex-con and a right wilted one at that!"

As soon as he struck her, he bitterly regretted it and the well of tenderness he had for her immediately overflowed.

"I'm sorry, hen. I'm sorry." He tried to take her into his arms but she knocked him aside and sent Agnes running to phone for the police. When the police came, she had him charged with assault.

He marvelled at the long memories and the natural vindictiveness of women. Madge had never forgiven him for playing the field and it did not matter what he did or did not do now, it made no difference. She continued to punish him at every opportunity and all the misfortunes that befell them were fuel for the fire of her resentment.

Sometimes he felt he could not stand the camp, the Nissen hut, or Madge any longer, and he took the tram to Springburn and stood at his old street corner and watched the world go by. Often he would meet someone who had once been a customer, or a neighbour or a friend and they would buy him a drink and talk about old times, or the war, or the present.

Then one day he met Sammy Hunter. He could never fathom how Sammy of all people had been a conscientious objector. He certainly did not fit in with most people's idea of what a pacifist should look like. Sammy had the appearance of a prize fighter with his stocky aggressive build and broken nose and short red hair. He came from a military family. All his brothers had been in the Army and his father had once been a sergeant-major. He remembered how Sammy's father used to drill all the wee Hunters in Springburn Park and children from miles around came to jeer at them. It occurred to him that this could be why Sammy refused to have anything to do with the military. He would probably have been sick to death of army ways long before the war started.

Sammy shook him warmly by the hand and thumped his arm as if he were genuinely glad to see him.

"How are you doing, Alec? Where are you staying? I never see you around Springburn now. Come on up to the house. I've got some beer in."

He accepted the invitation but once in Sammy's wee room and kitchen the memory of Sammy's wife, Ruth, hit him with depressing pain. He saw the photograph of her on the mantelpiece. Many a time he had come to collect the insurance money and admired that sexy beauty. He sighed and jerked his head towards the photo.

"She was a lovely girl. You were a lucky man."

"I know."

Sammy poured out the beer and pushed a glass towards Alec and Alec's hand reached out for it then suddenly drew back again.

"I was with her that night. She was fed up and lonely and I took her to the pictures. We had just sat down when the air-raid started. I tried to get her out, Sam."

The night when the Ritzy Cinema was destroyed by a direct hit came roaring at him through time to make him cringe. He felt sick.

"I was going to take her back home. We were on our way to the exit . . . Afterwards I clawed at the place with my bare hands. I tried my damndest to get her out but the fact remains if I hadn't have taken here there she would still be alive."

A nerve twitched at Alec's face in the silence that followed. Then Sammy said:

"It was the war. Dessie Street got it as well. If she had been there . . ." He shrugged. "Drink your beer."

"But I was with her."

Sammy paused before going on.

"I've had this horror of her dying alone among strangers. It's over five years ago now but it still bugged me, the thought of her being alone and frightened when it happened. She always liked you. I'm glad you were there."

Alec sighed again.

"Such a bloody waste, isn't it? And I bet the Jerries'll be better off than us now. Look at me. No job. No home. Squatting in bloody Nissen huts. I admit I didn't give much thought to why I went away to fight, but, my God, Sammy, it wasn't for this. Sometimes I wonder what it was all about. Oh, I know what they tell us, but politicians tell so many bloody lies."

"I'm reading this book just now. It says there's a sickness in Western civilisation and it's from that that both Fascism and the war grew. It's a wrong way of looking at human beings. It's the materialistic view. The idea that men are only valued in economic terms, and to the extent they submerge with their group or class, or nation, and make its ends their ends."

Alec took a swig of beer.

"Sounds like Fascism. But we're supposed to have beaten that."

"Don't you believe it. No, we've got to get an entirely new angle of approach to problems, Alec. We've got to reassert the value of the dignity and the rights of the individual. And we can't do that by holding an atomic bomb over their heads. We've got to build up an international morality and it's got to be supported by spiritual forces. Christ, Mohammed, Buddha, Confucius—they've all something worthwhile to teach us."

"I don't think there's any danger of another war, though. Nobody would use an atomic bomb."

"What are you talking about, man? They already have— twice. There were so many men, women, children and animals buried in Hiroshima and Nagasaki, they haven't been able to make an accurate count. And a so-called civilised Western nation did that. How about when they all have the bomb? And they will."

"You're a right cheerful Charlie."

"Just facing facts. I believe, you see, Alec, that now is the time to fight for the peace. Now is the time to prevent

174

the worst war of all. This is the fight for real survival right now!"

"To hell! I think I'll leave this fight to the weans. They've a lot more energy than me now."

"You had another one, the last I heard. How many does that make?"

"Seven."

"Seven? Some guys have all the luck."

"Call that luck? Och, they're a great bunch but, my God, Sammy, they've got mouths like Hoovers and they're growing out of all their clothes. If I don't get work soon I don't know what I'll do."

"At least they'll get dinners and milk at school now and there's going to be family allowances. That should help."

"Thank God for all of it but all the same I'm desperate for a job. It's slow death hanging about like this."

"Well, Joe Banks where I work is due to retire soon. I could put in a good word for you. But it's not in the office, Alec. It's not your kind of job . . ."

"Listen, mate, I don't care what kind of job it is as long as it's a job."

"Joe's the storeman. He works in the basement. As I said, it's . . ."

"Do you think there's a chance?"

"I don't see why not. I'll certainly do my best."

Alec got up, grabbed Sammy's hand and, speechless with gratitude, pumped it energetically up and down.

Sammy laughed.

"Take it easy. Where did you say you were living? I'll speak to the boss tomorrow and come out at night and tell you what he says. He'll probably let me know when you can go in and see him."

"Hughenden Playing Fields, off Great Western Road. It's right next to the asylum. Handy if I go berserk. They can just toss me across the fence. I'm itching to tell Madge, Sammy." He made for the door. "See you tomorrow, then."

He clattered down the stone stairs with almost as much

175

vigour as he once had after seeing Ruth. Now he did not look back at the window as he used to but winged his way across to the camp as fast as the tramcar and his long legs would carry him.

"Where the hell have you been?" Madge greeted him above the racket of all the children. "You've been drinking again. I smell the stink of you from here."

"Och, I only had a bottle of beer, hen."

"Only? The money for that could have bought the weans something, you rotten selfish bastard!"

"Now just a minute, Madge. Give us a chance."

"I gave you your chance years ago. And look where it's got me."

He groaned.

"I met Sammy Hunter. He took me up to his house."

"What did you do there? Compare notes with him about his wife?"

"Once and for all, Madge, will you shut up about Ruth. She was a nice girl."

"Oh, she was a nice girl, was she? I'll 'nice girl' you!" She flung herself at him, her fingers digging and grabbing and shaking him, her face ugly and contorted.

He struggled with her and all the children began to scream and jump around them. Desperately he bawled at her.

"I've got the chance of a job, you maniac! In Sammy's place. He's coming here tomorrow night to fix it up."

"Oh, so you think you'll soon be back to your f——ing cocky self, do you, in an office full of girls, do you? You think you're going to leave me here in this dump with this howling mob all day, do you?"

"Madge, for God's sake!"

"Well, I'll soon fix you. I'll tell Sammy a thing or two for a start and if you do get the job I'll go up there and barge into the place every day . . ."

All the time she was fighting him and it took all his strength to keep a grip on her arms or wrists.

"Agnes!" she shouted. "Sadie! He's twisting my arms. He's hurting me. Run quick and phone the police!"

"Madge, what are you trying to do to me? I'm trying to get you and the weans out of here. This is the first chance I've got."

She gave him a punch on the shoulder that made him stagger back.

"You've had your chance. Now it's my turn. You stay here. You watch your own weans. I'll find a job. I'll go out and work."

She seemed hell-bent on destroying him. Finishing him off good and proper. Grinding him under her big strong foot as if he were no more than an insect.

"After I come out the nick again, you mean?"

She laughed then and it was the big blowzy laugh that did it. He suddenly lashed out at her with all his strength, all his pent-up frustrations.

Afterwards, running through the quiet dark streets where Madge had often walked admiring the houses, he sweated with the thought that he might have killed her if it had not been for the children all hanging desperately on to him like leeches and the sound of Charlie's sobbing voice, high-pitched and pleading with fear.

"Daddy! Daddy! Daddy!"

He stopped running eventually and slipped in behind some bushes in the driveway of a house. He was shaking and gasping for breath and the nightmare scene he had left still imprisoned him like a shroud of icy cobwebs.

It had been raining and the leaves of the bushes had an earthy smell and glistened and dripped with water. The dampness seeped through him and made him shudder as he peered through the leaves. The big villa was in darkness. Maybe the owners were out enjoying themselves at the theatre, or away on holiday. Staring at the place, it occurred to him how ill-divided the world was. What made these people so special that they had so much of the world's goods and comforts and he had so little?

Was the man who owned that house or any of the other men around here such paragons of virtue? Did they work harder than he had once worked? Were they more honest?

He had never stolen a thing in his life but now for the first time he was really tempted. If he took something from that house what would it mean to the owner who owned so much, compared with how valuable, how important, what a difference it could make to himself who had nothing.

Perhaps there was enough money in a safe in there to give to a house-factor as "key money". Money could get anything. If he had enough money he could get a house, a decent house. Not unnecessarily big like that one but adequate—a good-sized flat in Springburn with a bathroom in one of the decent red sandstone buildings—maybe up the Balgray Hill near the park.

The poky room and kitchen in Cowlairs Pend had been smaller than the Nissen hut.

He was still in the nightmare, he could still hear Charlie's voice. The dream of money and a house only spun across the surface for a minute and then was gone with the temptation, leaving him more tormented than ever.

He ached to run again. He could thumb lifts down south on the long-distance lorries. He could get to London. He could shake free of Madge and the weans and all his problems, no bother at all. He could manage fine on his own.

The prospect of absolute freedom, the chance to start life afresh, reared up with tantalising attractiveness. It immediately lightened him, seemed to lift the weight of the whole world off his shoulder.

He moved, restless to be away. The bushes rustled and sprayed his crumpled demob suit with water.

He said a mental goodbye to Madge and the weans. He saw them all in his mind's eye.

He wiped his wet face with the sleeve of his jacket as he walked away. Then, still rubbing clumsily at his face and cursing himself, he turned back towards the camp.

# Chapter Twenty-One

Catriona began reading psychology books. She read about things like transference and wondered if that explained Melvin's behaviour. Was he transferring everything about himself on to her? When he accused her of being weak and no use—was he secretly afraid of facing his own weaknesses and guilt feelings? And if so, what could she do about it? She was becoming more and more convinced that either Melvin and the old man were going off their heads, or she was. She felt herself slipping, losing her grasp, as if she were hanging on to the edge of a precipice and below her yawned a black pit.

At every opportunity she studied the Bible in an effort to cling on.

She read every paper or magazine that had a horoscope. Her ears were for ever attuned to anything that might apply to her problems on the radio, or in anyone's casual conversation. She read the agony columns but no one's agony seemed so complicated and hopeless as her own.

Everything was getting beyond her. The housework was a nightmare roundabout on which she whirled round and round without end. And Melvin still kept trying to involve her in all the problems and extra responsibilities that success was bringing to the business.

Her father-in-law worried her to distraction but Melvin pooh-poohed the idea that the old man needed a doctor.

"Da and I aren't like you, with your pills and potions and your carry on with doctors. I don't want you bringing any of your doctors into my house. Da's old and can't hold his liquor so well now, that's all."

But Melvin did not see the old man as often as she did. Melvin was at the bakehouse half the night and it was then Da was at his worst and she did not know what to do. During the day for the most part he was perfectly all right. He never worked in the shop or the bakehouse now but occasionally called in to see how they were doing. Or he would ask Melvin for all the news at mealtimes. Then Catriona would wonder if she had imagined every night-time when she lay sick with exhaustion, and ears straining up from her pillow, listening for the old man.

Was that him staggering about the house again? Might he not fall down the stairs? It was not the first time he bumped down the stairs and hurt himself. Was that the scrape of a match, the crackle of flames?

Rigid with anxiety she made desperate plans of how she would rescue the children if Da set the house on fire and they suddenly became trapped in a roaring furnace. A thousand times in her imagination she wakened them. Should she risk precious seconds waiting until they put on their dressing-gowns, or should she try to rush them out the window and down the drain-pipe and put them in danger of catching pneumonia through being outside in the cold wearing only pyjamas?

But they would never be able to climb down drain-pipes from this height and neither would she. They would fall and break a leg or an arm, or be killed.

She wept to herself, but quietly, so that she could still listen.

Sometimes the old man called her and she jumped out of bed and raced to his room, tugging on her dressing-gown as she went, tightly knotting her nerves and emotions along with her dressing-gown cord, retaining a quiet voice although her heart drummed noisily.

"Yes, Da?"

"Take Tam out of here."

"Tam?"

"Tam MacGuffie. You remember Tam. There he is at the back of my bed."

Tam had been one of the Dessie Street bakers and he had been killed in the air-raid.

"There's nobody there, Da," she said. "Cuddle down and try to go to sleep."

His goatee beard bristled and he slavered with anger.

"It's all very well for you to talk. The wee nyaff's no taking up half your bed." He suddenly whipped back the bedclothes to reveal spindly legs dangling from a too short nightshirt. "I'm getting up!"

She averted her eyes in embarrassment and then was sickened to hear the thud of him falling on the floor. Rushing forward, she struggled to lift him. He seemed only a bundle of jaggy bones and yet felt as if he weighed a ton. It took every last ounce of her strength to wrench him up and stagger with him to the bed and while doing so she felt her menstrual period, which had just finished, start again with a painful gush. She felt faint and saw the old man through a misty haze.

"Are you all right?" she asked.

"What are you doing in my room?" he whined querulously. "I never get a minute's peace. It's terrible."

Sometimes she went to his room and he would be up and dressed and would immediately pounce on her.

"About time too. What's the meaning of this? I've been sitting here the whole day without a bite to eat or even a cup of tea."

"But, Da, this is the middle of the night," she'd wail. "You had your tea hours ago."

But there would be no convincing him and she would have to trail downstairs and wander about the kitchen half asleep cooking ham and eggs or sausage or whatever she could find, then carry it up on a tray to his room.

Sometimes by the time she got there he would be back in bed and asleep and if she wakened him he would peer incredulously at the ham and eggs and sausage, and yelp in high-pitched outrage.

"Have you gone off your bloody nut? It's the middle of the night!"

More often than not he would have fallen on to the floor off his chair. She was suspended in continuous terror of his falling into the fire, of opening his door and having to face the most appalling, horrific sight.

As it was, to watch his slow disintegration was bad enough. On the wall he had a picture of himself as a spruce, straight-backed young man and every time she saw it, then looked at the tottering, red-eyed, white-haired old wreck of a man, depression destroyed her a little.

Was this what we all have to come to? she wondered. Was this all there was to life? All the worry, the pain, the struggling, the trying to understand—it was all for this?

She sought to keep her eyes averted from the picture. She tried to look at, yet not see, the old man, to find some secret place within herself, if not in the house, where she could be free of distress, but there was nowhere.

The old man began to dominate her whole life, to take up all her time and energies to the exclusion even of caring for the children, and Catriona felt sad to think that the children's childhood was passing away and she had no longer the patience or the time for them. It became a regular job to heave Da off the floor in the middle of the night and half carry him back into bed, and somehow the menstrual period that had come back that first time never quite dried up. It streamed heavier each month and heavier and heavier in between months, until it seemed her life's blood was flowing fast away.

In terror that Melvin would find out, she planned another visit to the doctor. To withstand a repeat of Melvin's obscene tirade about going to see the doctor was impossible.

She began to watch him from the corner of her eye when

he did not know she was looking. She furtively listened at the door of any room he was in. For self-protection she tried harder and harder to appear normal when she was with him, as if nothing at all was the matter. Often she chatted about trivial things and laughed while dishing up meals in the dining-room. Then she would come through to the kitchen to the cupboard in the corner for more plates and weep helplessly in shadows behind the door with her arms sprawled over the shelves and her head rolling.

Then eventually, waiting in the doctor's surgery, she was strung up in an anguish of suspense in case Melvin somehow found out where she was. Her turn came and she poised herself on the edge of the chair at the opposite side of the doctor's desk. He looked almost as old as her father-in-law.

The wrinkled mouth under the tufty grey moustache still strained back to reveal the same little yellow teeth. She stared at him without hope. She felt so terrible and it was all so complicated and she was so tired, she did not know where to begin.

It occurred to her that the people who most needed help might often be the least likely to get it. For one reason or another they might not be able to communicate their condition in either an adequate way or a way that would arouse enough sympathy and understanding.

She did not feel well enough to explain. Her mind had gone blank. She did not know where to begin. She heard herself murmur apologetically about having heavy periods and being tired all the time when a loud buzz at the front doorbell made her jump and burst into tears.

"It's maybe my husband!" She screwed herself up, hands to mouth, eyes enormous, terrified, waiting, listening to the sound of the receptionist plodding across the carpeted hall outside, listening to the door opening, listening to the muffled voices.

The doctor said, "It's only another patient."

And he gave a jerky little giggle.

She froze inside. She hated him almost as much as she hated Melvin.

Now he was writing a prescription. He was rising. She rose too.

She thought, "Any minute now he's going to say—'It's just nerves.'"

He smiled. She smiled.

"It's just nerves," he assured her, seeing her to the door and shaking her politely by the hand before ushering her out.

On the slow way home, like a little old woman bent against pain, walking carefully, she tried to take deep breaths to sooth herself.

She thought, "Where can I go? What can I do?"

Turning into Botanic Crescent she passed her next-door neighbours, the minister's house. His name was Reverend John Reid and he was Mrs Vincent's father. Her feet faltered, halted, then returned to Reverend Reid's house. Heart pounding at the enormity of what she was doing she tugged at the doorbell.

She had never had anything to do with the Reids. Occasionally they smiled in passing and Reverend Reid lifted his hat but they had never exchanged more than half a dozen polite words of conversation about the weather. She had certainly never been in the Reids' house.

Now she gazed in consternation at the prim elderly maid who opened the door.

"I . . . I was wondering if I could see Mr Reid?"

"What?" The maid screwed up her face and strained one ear forward.

"Could I see the minister please? It's terribly important."

"You're the woman from next door, aren't you?"

"Yes. I want to ask the minister's advice about something Is he in?"

The older woman moved back and somewhat grudgingly allowed Catriona to enter. "I'll see. Wait here."

Left standing in the hall after the maid plodded slowly

away into one of the rooms Catriona stared apprehensively around. The rosewood hall with its turkey-red carpet gleamed darkly and somehow made her feel out of time as well as place. Her nerves twitched and her thoughts raced but opposite the grandfather clock slowly tick-tocked, its heavy brass pendulum lazily, contentedly, swinging.

Knotting her hands together she strained her eyes and ears in an attempt to decipher words from the low murmur of voices coming from the room. She thought she heard a woman say something like, "Not one of your flock", but could not be sure. One thing she did catch was the gentle sighing tones of long-suffering resignation.

Then the maid reappeared followed by a determinedly smiling Mrs Reid.

"Good afternoon, Mrs MacNair. Do come in. Jessie tells me you wish to speak to my husband. We were just about to go out but . . ."

"Oh, please," Catriona interrupted. "Don't let me detain you. I'm so sorry for intruding like this."

The portly figure of Reverend Reid sailed towards her with outstretched hand.

"Not at all. Sit down, my dear. Duty comes first."

His wife's smile was like a pain.

"I'll see about a cup of tea."

"No, no, please, I'd rather you didn't," Catriona pleaded.

"All right, if you insist." The ladylike smile again and the polite little tilt to the head that reminded Catriona of Mrs Vincent. "I'll leave you to talk in private."

"Thank you," Catriona murmured. Then after the older woman left she sat staring down at her hands.

"Well, my dear?" the minister prompted gently. "What seems to be the trouble?"

Catriona wished she had never come. People in this kind of district did not do this kind of thing. The "done thing" here was to keep up a respectable front at all costs. One did not talk about intimate things to strangers or neighbours, even if the strangers and neighbours were people of the Church.

By seeking help she was only making herself more of an outcast. It occurred to her that Melvin, by managing to keep up his front of normality for outsiders, would gain sympathy from these people without even trying.

For the first time she felt class conscious, even though, in a small way, Melvin was still a business man. Like his father before him he could make and hang on to money and this alone gained him respect and acceptance.

Catriona's background had been the working class, where people borrowed and shared everything including their most intimate troubles.

"It's nothing really." She struggled to bring some dignity and pride into her voice. "Actually I haven't been feeling too well and everything seems to have been getting on top of me."

"Ah, well, yes." Reverend Reid leaned back in his chair and began gently tapping the arm of it with his fingertips. "It happens to all of us at some time or other. Perhaps a visit to your doctor, my dear. I'm sure he would be able to give you a tonic."

"Yes, of course!" Catriona said brightly. "How stupid of me. I should have gone there. Of course!" She blinked and blinked again but despite her efforts to be brave and discreet, tears were escaping and coursing down her face and her mouth was twisting and quivering out of control.

"My dear!" Reverend Reid murmured unhappily.

"It's my father-in-law. He's so much work. I'm up in the middle of the night with him. He does all sorts of stupid and dangerous things. I can't stand it much longer."

"Poor old soul! You must ask God to help you to be patient, Mrs MacNair. Old age is something that comes to all of us. You'll be old yourself one day, my dear, and you'll want your children to be loving and patient with you."

"It's my husband, too." She knew she was only making things worse but could not help blurting out the truth.

"I've come to hate him. I can't help it. He nags at me day and night. You've no idea what he's like. Nobody has. I tried to leave him but he came after me acting like a maniac, banging his head on the wall and threatening to kill himself.'

"Oh, dear, dear." The minister tutted. "Poor soul. He was a prisoner of war, wasn't he?"

"Yes, but . . ."

"God alone knows what the poor fellow must have suffered."

She took deep breaths. Then she said:

"You think I'm neurotic and selfish."

"My dear," he soothed. "Life cannot be easy for you. I'll pray that God will strengthen you, and help you to find enough love and patience to carry you through this little difficult patch." He sighed. "Try to feel thankful that you have your husband safely home beside you, my dear. My poor grandson was killed. Think how his wife must feel."

She rose stiffly and immediately.

"How dreadful of me. I forgot about your tragedy. I'm so terribly sorry."

"Reggie was . . ." The old man shook his head, unable to speak for a minute. "Reggie was a fine boy."

"Yes, he was."

Pleasure illuminated his face. "You knew him?"

"I met him a couple of times. I thought he was a perfect gentleman and very, very handsome."

"Yes, wasn't he? Yes, wasn't he, indeed?"

"I'd better not take up any more of your time when you're going out. Thank you for being so kind."

"Not at all. Not at all."

He patted her shoulder as he saw her to the door.

"Your husband's a fine brave man, too. Just give him time, my dear. These have been difficult years for all of us."

Immediately she got into the privacy of her own house

she leant her head against the door and wept loudly and broken-heartedly.

Her problem was becoming more and more a physical one. She was bleeding so constantly and heavily that every day was an ordeal of exhaustion to be overcome.

She got to the stage when she knew something would have to be done. If she were to survive, the odds against her would have to be cut down.

"Melvin!" she burst out eventually. "Something will have to be done about Da."

"What do you mean, 'Something will have to be done about Da'?"

"He'll have to go into a home."

Melvin's eyes bulged. "Toss my father out on to the street?" he shouted. "I'll see you out on the street first!"

"I didn't say toss your father out on to the street. I said —a home—or a hotel."

"He's got a home. I gave him a home."

She tried to sound reasonable.

"I can't help it, Melvin. I'm sorry."

"What do you mean, you're sorry? I've a big ten-roomed house here and you expect me to turf my father out. You're rotten selfish, that's your trouble. Nobody matters but yourself."

"I just don't feel able to look after Da any more. I can't go on like this. I just can't. He's too much for me."

Melvin's mouth twisted.

"Aw, shut up, you're always the same. Whine, whine, whine! What have you ever done for Da?"

"I've done my best. That's what I've done. Now he'll have to go."

"What do you mean, 'He'll have to go'? I promised my father he would never have anything to worry about as long as he had me. And my word's my bond."

"You had no right."

"What do you mean—I had no right? He's my father."

"And I'm your wife."

188

"So? I've given you a good home here as well, haven't I? What more do you want? Buckingham Palace and a squad of maids?"

"I want your father out of here so that I can have a rest. I've the children to think of."

"The children!" he scoffed. "You don't care about them any more than you care about my father. You're always narking on at them. You make their life a bloody misery."

She stared at him in heartbroken silence for a minute or two. Had it become so bad, so noticeable? Were the children actually suffering, really unhappy?

Melvin grabbed a newspaper, shoved it up between them, shut her out, ended the conversation.

Her lips trembled.

"Are you or are you not going to do something about your father?"

"Aw, shut up!"

She left the room and went for her coat. She went out, shutting the front door quietly. Her mind was in a daze.

Walking slowly, painfully down on to Queen Margaret Drive she tried to sort out what she could do. If she left again it could not be to her mother's. Her mother had never forgiven her for going back to Melvin the last time. And, as if she knew that it was the last time Catriona would stay there, she had turned the full force of her emotions on Rab. They were never apart now. Sometimes Hannah called for him at the bakehouse and they went straight from there to the pictures. They still argued and fought but it was as if they did not know how else to speak. It was a kind of passion that blotted everyone else out, including Catriona.

She would need to find someplace else to live, somewhere for the children to sleep and eat and have shelter. If she could find a job she could perhaps make enough money to pay for a place. But no, she knew that she would never be able to make enough money to pay rent and buy food and all that the children needed although if she had been able she would have tried. She was not able, that was the problem. She felt ill. Every now and again pain possessed her, then left her weak and nearly collapsing with relief after it faded away. Recently it had been getting worse.

She marvelled at how lucky men were, how much suffering they missed.

Reaching Great Western Road, she hesitated as if lost. Then, remembering that Madge was living in an old RAF camp further along the road, she forced herself to go in a slow plodding pace in that direction.

Madge was standing outside her Nissen hut with her big arms folded across her chest. Charlie was staggering about nearby and some of the other children were shouting and playing and racing back and forth, often knocking Charlie down.

"Hello, hen," Madge greeted her. "Come on in. It's ages since I've seen you. That marvellous house of yours just makes me jealous." She gave a big cheery laugh. "You're a lucky wee midden, eh? Sit down, the chair won't bite you."

"I don't feel very lucky," Catriona ventured.

"Well, you should."

"But, Madge. I'm terribly worried." She gave a hasty glance around then lowered her voice. "It's my periods. They're so heavy—they go on all the time. I feel terrible."

Madge scratched herself then tucked her hair behind her ear.

"Drink plenty milk stout."

"Milk stout?"

Madge laughed.

"What are you looking so shocked for? It makes blood, doesn't it?"

"Does it?"

"Och, anybody knows that. They give it to women in hospitals."

"Do they?"

"You get your man to buy some bottles and take it regular."

Catriona nibbled at her lip. She did not feel as if she were getting to the root of the problem.

"It's not just that. My father-in-law seems to be going off his head. Half the time he imagines he's still in Dessie Street. He gets all mixed up. Especially at night. That's the funny thing about it. He's mostly all right during the day when Melvin's in. But at night it's awful. I never know what he's going to be like.

"Och, the poor old soul. It'll be his dotage. It comes to all of us, hen." Another big laugh shook Madge's chest. "Any more complaints, eh? You're a scream, hen. There you are along in Botanic Crescent among all the toffs in a lovely big house with a good man. And here I am with damn all. And you come here trying to tell me your troubles!"

Catriona flushed.

"I suppose it does sound ridiculous. I'm sorry, Madge."

"You look a right toff yourself. You suit your hair up like that. My God, some folk have all the luck. You're even made wee and dainty and, as Julie would say, tairably, tairably refined. Think yourself lucky, hen. That's my advice. You go back home tonight and think yourself damned lucky!"

Catriona tried to graft a look of cheerfulness across her face.

"All right, Madge. I will. Talking about Julie—I wonder how she's getting on? I don't suppose she wrote to you, did she? I wrote to Mr Gemmell and enclosed a letter for Julie and asked him to post it to her address in England. But I've never had any reply. I wrote to her father again and never got any reply from him either. He must have gone with her. I can't understand it, can you? I hope she's all right."

"Och, she'll be all right," Madge said. "She looks as if she can take damned good care of herself, that one!"

191

# Chapter Twenty-Two

Mrs Vincent had come every day without fail to the hospital. Julie had written to Botanic Crescent right away and told her where to come, and she had headed the letter "Dear Mum" and ended it—"Your loving daughter, Julie". She did not know why she had written like that. She always called her Mrs Vincent to her face and often went to no pains to hide the fact that she did not like her very much.

She was sure Mrs Vincent had no great love for her either, and she always felt that at any minute she would disappear from her life. She kept thinking to hell with her and good riddance. Yet every day Mrs Vincent arrived exactly on time and brought fruit and flowers and chocolates.

Julie kept saying, "You shouldn't have. I don't need anything. I'm all right. When I want something I'll buy it for myself."

But she looked forward to each visit because she trembled with eagerness to show off the baby.

"Isn't she a doll? An absolute doll." She held the little bundle with great tenderness, savouring every silky flower-petal feel of it against her breast, studying every hair on its downy head, rubbing her cheek gently against the vulnerable softness, closing her eyes with love that was like a pain. "She's so beautiful, isn't she? So good, too. Look at her. Look how she just lies there without making a sound."

The fingers of Mrs Vincent's gloved hand eased back the shawl. Then she smiled and murmured agreement and before sitting down tickled the tiny chin with one finger.

"Coochie-coochie coo! They are sweet when they're tiny!"

Julie had bristled at the word "they" as if it somehow detracted from her baby's uniqueness. No other baby in the universe was as exquisitely wonderful as her daughter.

She would never forget the first time she saw her. It had been as if she had gone in through one door of a torture chamber and eventually struggled out another and found herself changed as a result. From the moment she looked at her baby she knew she would never be the same person again.

A new part of her had been tempered in the fire of pain, was hypersensitive, had subtle nuances, strange penetrations of feeling that had never been dreamed of before.

Looking at her new-born child she saw her own flesh, a completely vulnerable part of herself yet with none of her faults or imperfections. When the child cried she cringed inside and palpitated with the acuteness of her concern.

All the time she kept staring at the baby. With great care and wonderment her eyes studied the tender pink bulge of the cheek, the rosebud mouth, the little creased neck that seemed too thin, the dimpled fists. Any movement, a sucking twitch of the mouth, the slow enchanting opening of the eyes to stare straight at her, touched on ready ripened nerves like an orgasm.

All the time they kept telling her that it would be best if it were adopted and she had agreed before the baby was born. But now seeing it, now being different, she no longer could decide what ought to be done for the best. Just to think of giving the little girl away made her stomach immediately plummet down as if she had stepped into an empty lift shaft.

She kissed the baby and kissed it again and cuddled away underneath the bedclothes with it in her arms so that no one could see her weeping. She wished she could ask the child what it wanted. In the dark tunnel of the bed-clothes, through rainbow tears she kissed the milky mouth and longed to be able to converse with it.

They said it was not fair on the child to have only one

193

parent. A child needs a father as well as a mother, they said.

There was this well-off couple up north just longing for a child, they told her. They had a lovely big house out in the country and if they adopted the little girl she would lack for nothing.

Think of the difference, they said. What had she to offer? An overcrowded nursery during the day or someone looking after the baby while she was out at work. A room and kitchen in the Gorbals at night. Not even a garden. Nowhere for a pram.

Then when the child grew up—what could she say about its father?

Holding and kissing and nursing it, her face soaking the pillow, she thought, "If only she knew me now. If only she could remember. If only she could know how much I love her."

But maybe it was better that her daughter should never have any memory of her at all.

How could she bear the child to know that her father had been some faceless airman who had picked her drunken Gorbals mother off the street, and afterwards disappeared? She did not even know his name or what he looked like.

She tried to clean her mind of the memory of that night and the terrible shame in case just thinking about it in the presence of her baby might in some way contaminate it.

She knew she could never endure her daughter knowing about her and being ashamed of her.

The adopting parents were such *respectable* people, they said.

She could almost see them. They had a neat villa in the suburbs of Aberdeen or Inverness or Oban. Probably their parents had helped them to buy it. They had a big garden, of course, and a car and they went regularly to church on Sundays. They were known and respected members of the community. He played golf and she was a member of the

Women's Guild. They had a joint account in the local bank. They fitted securely into all the accepted patterns.

Julie closed her eyes and prayed to them.

"Please, please, be good and loving and kind and patient and understanding always and always to my little girl."

She did not allow Mrs Vincent to come for her on the day she left the hospital, but she promised to visit her at Botanic Crescent the day after.

She did not want anyone to be there when she said goodbye to her baby.

In front of Mrs Vincent she had always managed to maintain a brusque, cheerful exterior.

At visiting times they gossiped and laughed as if she had come to hospital for no more than the simple uncomplicated removal of an appendix.

If Mrs Vincent noticed the tragic eyes, and the face puffy and swollen with weeping, she never once mentioned it.

The last day came and panic swooped inside Julie like the big dipper at the fair.

She kept telling herself that this was not, could not be, the last time she would ever see her baby. She would never know her daughter. Never see her in all the stages of growing up, never know her as a woman. And her daughter would never know her! Shaking and weak and bewildered, Julie tried to console herself. Her baby would go to the adopting parents now but at the end of a few weeks she could still change her mind before signing the papers.

They told her:

"You'll be able to think more clearly once you get home and back to normal."

She held her daughter in her arms. She gazed at her face, tracing its each and every contour with her finger, then eased her finger into the little hand.

The nurse was impatient to be away.

"I'll have to take her now. You've just got to be brave."

"Sure, pal. Sure," Julie said, handing over the baby.

195

Then before she could snatch another look or touch or say the word goodbye, the nurse turned on her heel, clipped smartly down the corridor, and disappeared through swing doors.

Julie watched the doors wham backwards and forwards, then shudder, then become still. She lifted her case and wandered outside. Part of her heart and soul seemed to have been wrenched away. She felt incomplete. All her instincts were screaming out in protest. Bewilderment made her take the wrong turning. She thought she would never get home and she did not care.

Her father was standing at the corner as usual. On the outside it was as if nothing had happened. The Gorbals looked exactly the same. Yet had there been so many shops that sold prams or baby clothes or toys or baby food before? The sight of each shop tormented her. And each baby in its mother's arms and each child playing in the street were knives of anguish stabbing at her.

Her father had an old white scarf knotted at his neck and his cap pulled well down over his beaky face. He was shuffling from one foot to the other and rubbing and smacking at his hands and grinning.

"Hallo, there, hen. Ah've got the kettle on. The tea'll no' take a minute."

Off he scampered up the close to get everything ready as if she were just coming home as usual from work.

She took her time, her hand on the banister pulling herself up each stair.

"Ah've got a confession tae make," he said once she had arrived in the house, taken off her coat, and flopped helplessly into a chair. "Ah bumpt intae that pal o' yours—whit's her name? A bonny fair-headed wee lassie."

"Catriona?"

"Aye, that's the one. Well, ah was up the town the other day fur a message in Woolworth's and she collared me, hen. Ah couldni help it."

"You told her!"

"She kept asking me. Ah didni know whit tae say."

Julie sighed. "Oh, never mind. It can't be helped now."

"Here, drink yer tea, hen. That'll cheer you up. And you'll be glad of yer pal, tae. She'll be here in a minute. She wanted tae go and get you at the hospital but ah said you didni want anybody there. That was whit you said, wasn't it, hen?"

Julie sipped at her tea and did not answer. She was saving her energy for the bright brittle act she would have to put on while Catriona or anyone else was there.

"Och, never mind, hen." Her father hesitated, groping for words with which to comfort her about the child. "It's best this way. This way, y'see, you'll never know it."

Tears spurted out of her eyes of their own accord. They splashed down her face and trickled along her jaw and down into the hollows of her neck.

She went on sipping her tea, not saying anything.

"Och, dinni greet, hen. Them yins know what's best for you, ah'm sure. You're a young lassie yet, and bonnie tae. Now you'll be able to meet some nice fella and get married again eh? Fellas are no' so keen if there's somebody else's wean . . . There's the door, that'll be your pal now."

In obvious relief he scuttled off to let Catriona in.

Julie got up, clattered her cup down on the table and fumbled in her pockets for a handkerchief.

Surprise at the changed appearance of Catriona momentarily switched her attention away from her own problems. Catriona's fair hair was now plaited and circled her head like a little crown. She had always been small but she had lost weight and her delicate bone structure was more noticeable She had acquired a fragile look with white skin drawn tight over her cheekbones casting dark shadows under her eyes.

In a way, although the colouring was completely different and they did not really look like one another at all, Catriona suddenly reminded Julie of Mrs Vincent.

They both seemed to possess the same genteel West End aura.

"There's a cup of tea in the pot if you want it," she told Catriona brusquely and then raised an eyebrow in her father's direction. "What the hell are you hanging about with a face like that for? Either sit down and content yourself or get away out the road."

"Aye, aw right. I'll away, hen. Cheerio the now."

The outside door banged shut. Then Catriona said:

"Oh, Julie!"

"Well? Do you want a cup of tea?"

Catriona sank gently into a chair and nodded as if she could not trust herself to speak.

"Before you start quizzing me," Julie said, "I'll confess all. He was crazy about me. I was crazy about him. But he's married and can't get a divorce so we had to call it a day and that's him out of the picture. They've advised me to have my baby adopted. They say it's best from the baby's point of view. A little girl, by the way, an absolute doll."

She grabbed her handbag, found her cigarettes, lit one and breathed deeply at the smoke. Then she took out her powder compact and energetically powdered her face.

"You can't," Catriona said.

"Can't what, pal?"

"Give your baby away. You'll never be able to forget her, Julie. She'll always be part of you. If you do this it'll torment you for the rest of your life."

"This has nothing to do with you or anybody else. It's my decision and my decision alone."

"You've just told me you've been advised to have her adopted."

"They say to think of what's best for the baby. That's exactly what I'm going to do."

"I don't want to interfere . . ."

"Well, don't!"

"But I must say this. I believe no one can feel the same for a baby as its own mother."

"I know what I feel." Julie sent a stream of smoke darting across the room. "I don't need you to tell me how I feel. It's my baby's feelings I've got to think about, not my own."

"Julie, you could manage somehow."

"There you go again—talking about me—always from my angle."

"But are you sure . . ."

"Look, pal, I know you mean well, but drop it, will you? I've told you, this is something I've got to decide for myself."

"Does Mrs Vincent know?"

"She found out and came to see me at the hospital. I promised to go and visit her tomorrow."

"You must pop in and see me too when you're so near."

"Sure! Sure! How are you getting on these days? Business doing well?"

"Oh, yes. It's a good locality, you see."

"Oh, I see. Aiverybody's tairaibly, tairaibly refined and frightfully decent and all that. Not like in dirty, horrid, immoral old Gorbals!"

"I only meant that Byres Road was a busy main street so there's always plenty of passing trade as well as regular customers."

Julie laughed.

"Sure, pal! Sure! And your grand big house?"

"As big as ever," Catriona replied in a light, bright voice.

"And your husband?"

"Oh, very well, thank you."

"And your family?"

"Fine. Fine."

Suddenly Catriona got up.

"I shouldn't have come just now, Julie, I'm sorry. You're too soon out of hospital and have too much on your mind to be bothered with visitors. Please forgive me."

Julie dragged at her cigarette.

"Don't give it a thought. I'm fine."

"I'll see you tomorrow then? When you come to visit Mrs Vincent?"

"Sure! Sure!"

She saw Catriona to the door and waved cheerily before shutting it.

Then she returned to the kitchen and the tears immediately overflowed again and made her crumple into a chair and just sit listening to the clock ticking her life away. Then her father came back for his meal and she jumped up and flounced about on her high heels getting everything ready.

"Ah saw yer pal going away," her father said.

"Oh?"

"She was saying you're going over there tomorrow."

"I might. And then again—" Julie shrugged—"I might not!"

# Chapter Twenty-Three

"Catriona! Catriona! Catriona!"

The faint wailing came from upstairs.

"Mum, you should have seen me play football today," Fergus enthused. "Every time I got the ball I . . ."

"Oh, shut up!" she pleaded. "What do I care about football!"

"Catriona! Catriona! Catriona!"

Knocking Fergus aside she hurried upstairs sweating with weakness and nauseated by the sensation of raw liver slithering between her legs. More and more each day she had to increase the padding around herself, had to struggle with the difficulties of bathing and trying to retain some of her normal fastidiousness about personal hygiene.

"Catriona! Catriona! Catriona!"

"I'm coming, Da!"

She dare not visualise what she might find. Life was just carrying her on regardless, buffeting her about.

He was not in his room.

"Da! Where are you?"

She found him in the bathroom struggling with his braces. The stench was overpowering.

"Bloody diarrhoea!" he yelped. "Came on me so quick I've shitted my trousers."

It was then she noticed the mess of faeces on the bathroom floor and realised that there was a trail of it all the way from the bedroom. It was even on her shoes.

She willed herself not to retch.

"Came on so quick, y'see!" the old man whined. "I couldn't help it." He was shaking all over and staggering a little.

"It's all right, Da," she said. She was used to saying that. It had become a habit. "It's all right, Da," she always said, when it was not all right at all.

She felt ashamed. She was terrified someone might come to the door or even smell the house out in the street.

She must be something very loathsome in God's eyes. Now he seemed to be punishing her by rubbing her nose in dirt like an animal. If it was not stinking wet bedclothes it was this!

For a minute or two she just stood looking at the mess, her stomach heaving.

The old man managed to pull down his braces but his blue-veined shivering hands still refused to cope with the buttons of his fly.

She thought of calling to Fergus for help but checked herself. Fergus had a delicate stomach. He was easily nauseated; a hair, a chipped cup, a fly buzzing around the table could put him off his food. He would be ill if she brought him upstairs now.

She forced herself to go over and undo the buttons herself. She kept thinking:

"I'll never forgive Melvin for putting me and his father in this dreadful situation. I'll never forgive him. Never!"

The old man leaned on her and it took all her strength to hold his weight up while at the same time struggling to peel off the stinking trousers.

"I'll away to my bed now," he said. "This is terrible!"

"You can't go like that. You'll make the bedroom chairs and carpets and bedclothes all dirty. We'll get everything off and get you into the bath. You'll be all right."

She ran the bath, then with painful avoidance of the old man's eyes she stripped off the rest of his clothes, helped him across and half lifted him into the water. She sponged him down then dried him and hauled him out again. After wrapping the big towel round his skinny body she supported him as he stomped and staggered towards his room.

Then, armed with a pail of water and cloths and a bottle of disinfectant, she set about cleaning up the mess on all the floors. Tiny moans of distress escaped every now and again as the faeces stuck to her hands and splashed on to her clothes.

She felt God turning away from her, like her mother, with the same hatred, the same screwing up of the nose against something filthy and foul-smelling.

She harboured no resentment against the old man. Now that he too was weak and helpless and distressed it gave them something in common. But resentment was there, alternating in waves with her self-hate and misery, straining for release.

She kept thinking of Melvin. Their whole life together unrolled before her eyes. Every grievance she had ever nursed against him was remembered with bitterness. Especially the fact that when she had to get up early after a sleepless night, he lay on snoring for hours. He got enough sleep now all right. He knew how to take care of himself.

In her imagination she carried on long arguments with him and by the time she next saw him she was primed up ready at the drop of one wrong word to explode all the frustrations and hatreds of a lifetime on his head.

He was eating his breakfast when he remarked casually:

"Your pal doesn't seem to think much of you. Never even bothered to write and tell you why she didn't turn up."

"Julie isn't well just now, that's all. I'll hear from her. But it'll be no thanks to you—you and your rudeness and downright bad manners when my friends do come. You purposely try and discourage them. You're so selfish you want me just to be here on my own all the time, just pandering to your needs and being a slave to your precious house. You'd have me die alone here, alone and friendless, just as your first wife was."

His eyes bulged with shock.

"My Betty never wanted anyone else but me. You've gone off your nut."

She was trembling violently but she went over to him and stuck her face close to his, her eyes glittering, her facial muscles tense. "I'm not like your first wife!"

"I know," he retorted bitterly. "You couldn't be like her if you tried."

"You gave her a really marvellous funeral, didn't you? And you wanted plenty of people at that."

"All I did was make a passing remark about your pal not turning up and you suddenly, for no reason at all, go berserk about my Betty."

"You're not going to have any fancy funerals here for me."

"You're right there," he bawled back at her. "They can carry you out in a bloody orange box for all I care!"

"Oh, I know you don't care about me. I know you don't care if I never have anybody to talk to."

"What do you mean—" he began, but to his exasperation she suddenly burst into tears. "For God's sake! All I said was . . ."

"I know all you say," she sobbed. "I'm no use. I do nothing. Nothing!" She repeated the word as if she could not believe it. "Nothing!"

"It's no wonder I can't eat." His mouth twisted down and he jerked his plate away. "You're enough to put anybody off their food!"

"Your father could be dying. You don't even care about him."

"Now it's my father! Aw, shut up!"

Catriona could not reply because a sudden overpowering urge to vomit forced her to retreat to the privacy of the bathroom. She hung over the basin then slithered down on to the floor. She lay there for a long time before the pain and sickness passed and she was able to pull herself up as if out of a nightmare and return to the kitchen.

In the afternoon she made her way determinedly to the doctor's once more. Surely at least he would be able to give her something for her stomach and the bouts of pain that were fast becoming unendurable.

She rang the bell of his house in which he used a couple of rooms for surgery and waiting accommodation. The doctor himself opened the door, his little grin at the ready. It always surprised her how old he looked. But this time he looked shabby as well, in an old cardigan and reading-glasses and brown checked slippers.

"Good afternoon, Mrs MacNair."

"Good afternoon, Doctor." She hesitated on the doormat, longing to sit down and waiting for him to invite her in. But he waited, too, so she screwed up her face in pained embarrassed apology.

"I'm sorry to bother you, but I was hoping you'd give me something for my stomach. I'm not so bad at the moment but I have been awfully sick."

"If you come back tomorrow, certainly," he said. "This is my half-day."

"Oh." She stared helplessly at him. "I forgot."

"It's perfectly all right," he assured her before gently shutting the door.

She stood for a long time on the doormat suspended in a fog of lethargy. It seemed to her that she had reached a point of no return. She could not go on any longer.

Eventually she turned away and wandered about the streets in a daze before it occurred to her to go into a telephone booth, search for the number of a solicitor, and dial for an appointment.

At home they were all waiting impatiently for her.

"Where were you, Mum?" the boys queried. "What's for tea?"

"Did you remember my tobacco?" the old man wanted to know. "And where's my paper?"

"Where have you been all this time?" Melvin demanded indignantly.

Questions, questions, questions. She avoided their eyes, hid deep inside herself in case anyone might suspect what she had done and where she was going next day. Silently, she moved about making their meal and then listlessly leaned against the sink as she attended to the washing up.

"It's time you snapped out of it," Melvin said. "Pulled yourself together. You go about here like a half-shut knife. No wonder you're full of complaints. That's bad for you for a start—bad posture. You should always stand straight and keep your shoulders well back. It's all a question of willpower and physical jerks. I haven't so much time to do mine now but there's nothing to stop you from keeping fit. I'll show you a few really good exercises."

"It's a good sleep I need."

"Well, there's nothing to stop you from getting that."

"I'm up with your father every night."

"Well, that's your fault. You worry too much, that's your trouble. The old man takes a few nightcaps and you make a tragedy of it. Anybody would think it was the end of the world."

She turned and gazed sadly at him. Maybe it was the end of their world. She wanted to weep on his shoulder. But she knew the feeling of comfort and security in his arms would only be a illusion, a figment of her wishful thinking.

Just as she knew that although she desperately needed sleep, it would again be denied her.

This time she had to leap out of bed at the sound of the front door opening and closing. Dashing to the window she was horrified to see, by the light of the street lamps, the old man stomping along the crescent dressed in his striped pyjamas, his old black trilby and his working boots.

She stumbled about the room trying to dress rapidly and get out in time to catch him before he disappeared. Different catastrophes seesawed her mind. People in the crescent could see him and they would all be disgraced.

Or he could march straight into the river and be drowned.

She ran outside, her face twisted with the physical distress of movement.

Her father-in-law was nowhere to be seen.

Clutching her coat around her, Catriona hurried on to Queen Margaret Drive where she could see as far as Great Western Road. There was still no sign of him and she doubted that he would have been able to get any further.

Her overstretched nerves tied themselves in knots of apprehension. He must have gone down into the gardens. Running back, her eyes wide with panic, her mouth open and gasping for breath, she could see in her mind the brown bulging water of the river. In her imagination she plunged in to save the old man and drowned along with him, pulled down by his bony clinging fingers, and she sobbed out loud at the thought of the children being left without her.

The gate creaked open and she suddenly realised that it was dark and she was alone. She hesitated for a few seconds among the high bushes, wringing her hands and anxiously biting at her lip. Then she hurried down the steep steps to find the old man sprawled at the foot of them.

"Da?" She kneeled down beside him and he looked dazedly at her. "It's all right, Da. Come on. I don't care what Melvin says. I'm going to get the doctor," she said, although she had long ceased to believe that the doctor could do any good either for Da or herself.

They took ages struggling together to get up the slippery stone steps and back on to the crescent and into the house. Then she phoned the doctor and he promised, politely, to come as soon as he could.

It was morning before he arrived and she was still up making cups of tea and filling hot-water bottles for Da. Melvin had been told what had happened and he went to the old man's room, and stood pulling at his moustache and saying: "Anything you want or need, Da, just let me know. Anything at all!"

The doctor wrote out a prescription and chatted to Melvin, and asked about the business, and said he hoped the medicine would help his father but there was nothing much anybody could do now, and added:

"It's really just his age."

Afterwards Melvin said:

"He's no chicken himself. Quite a nice old guy, though. I don't mind you going to him."

"Thanks very much," she said bitterly. "Thanks for nothing!"

She returned upstairs to tell Da she was going out to get the medicine. She felt she was on a treadmill.

He seemed quite perky again.

"Strong as a horse," Melvin laughed. "He's wee but he's wiry. He'll last for years yet."

"My God," she thought. "My God!"

# Chapter Twenty-Four

Rain smeared all over Glasgow, enfolding it in a damp grey mist. It blurred Catriona's eyes as she walked. Edwardian and Victorian buildings loomed up, ghost-like, all around. Crowds of shadowy people stirred about.

She recalled a verse she had once read from a poem called "Glasgow" by Alexander Smith:

> City! I am true son of thine
> Ne'er dwelt I where great mornings shine
> Around the bleating pens
> Ne'er by the rivulets I strayed
> And ne'er upon my childhood weighed
> The silence of the glens.
> Instead of shores where ocean beats
> I hear the ebb and flow of streets.

She liked the poem. She loved Glasgow. She could imagine nothing better in the world than living here, having a flat to go to, somewhere in which she could feel safe, somewhere legally undisputably her own. Home, recognisable, everlasting, part of the great sea of Glasgow streets.

Dreams wafted about her mind like mist. They had no substance against the realities of pain and sickness and worry with which she was attempting to cope.

Everyone in the solicitor's plush carpeted office had treated her with attentive deference but she could not help wondering how much of it was due to her best clothes and her Kelvinside address. She was fast becoming aware of the yardstick of money that so many people used. Now she began to worry about how she was going to pay the solicitor's bill. She seemed only to be adding more problems to those she already had instead of solving them.

"And what can we do for you, Mrs MacNair?" The young solicitor's voice slid out like golden honey and he leaned forward to concentrate concern on her.

Her gaze flickered worriedly, uncertainly.

"I need help and advice."

"In a matrimonial problem, I believe."

"Yes."

She prayed for strength not to break down, not to sound selfish and neurotic. She prayed to be able to find the right words. And the right amount of words. Not too many. Not too few.

"I've been very unhappy for some time," she said slowly and carefully, her eyes clutching at the blotting-paper on the desk as if she were reading from it. "I feel my marriage is affecting my health. I feel that I have a duty to the children. I must get away and take them with me before they too are made miserable and ill."

"Were you thinking in terms of divorce or legal separation, Mrs MacNair?"

She looked up.

"I don't know. Divorce, I suppose."

His chair swung back and he caught himself by hitching his thumbs in his waistcoat.

"There are three main grounds for divorce—desertion, cruelty and adultery. Very briefly, the position with desertion is this. If you left your husband, he could keep offering you, in writing, a home with him. If you refused to accept his offers, then you would be in desertion and he could file divorce proceedings against you. This involves a period of three years."

"I would be the guilty party."

He spread out his hands.

"Technically, yes. Then there's adultery."

"As far as I know my husband has never committed adultery, so I suppose it would have to be cruelty."

"To make cruelty stand up in court you've got to have charged your husband on at least two occasions with assault. Then you would have police witnesses, etcetera, to back you up."

"I see." A bitter laugh jerked out. "That seems to be it, then."

The solicitor pursed his lips as if to say, "Pity!"

Hopelessness swamped her. Everywhere she turned it was the same.

"Of course, if you could get a note from your doctor to say that your marriage was affecting your health, Mrs MacNair, then we could at least attempt to prove justification in leaving so that you would not be the guilty party."

"If I left, what would I be entitled to take with me?"

"Your clothes. Articles given to you personally as gifts." He shrugged. "But, of course, you know what they say. Possession is nine-tenths of the law. If you managed to take more with you then it would be up to your husband to prove that the articles were his and that he was entitled to their return."

"I see. Oh, well." Smiling, Catriona gathered up her gloves and handbag. "I'll go and see my doctor and then I'll be in touch with you again. Not a very nice day, is it? So dull and wet."

"Indeed. Indeed." Cheerfully he leapt to his feet and made the door in a few energetic strides. "Going to be fog tonight, I think."

Back outside, rain mixed with perspiration and wetly covered her face. She felt as if she were drowning. The journey home to Botanic Crescent stretched before her, all-absorbing, like the lonely ascent of the highest and most perilous mountain in Scotland.

Straining herself along slowly and painfully she thought, "I'm going to die." She sensed death very near. It did not frighten her, but she felt a terrible sadness at the thought of never seeing her children again. She did not want to say goodbye to Glasgow, either. If she never felt any home belonged to her, at least she knew she belonged to Glasgow.

Her mind clung desperately to the city. Despite her physical weakness a tough core of spiritual strength remained.

> *I belong to Glasgow,*
> *Dear old Glasgow town,*
> *But there's something the matter with Glasgow*
> *For it's going round and round . . .*

In a daze she successfully reached Botanic Crescent, then, having reached it, remembered she had meant to go to the doctor's for the note. But the ordeal of another agonising journey and then the seemingly impossible task of convincing the doctor that she was ill proved too much for her. She suspected, too, that the doctor would not act in any way against Melvin without first discussing the matter with him. That would result in another terrible scene and she could not stand any more.

Fumbling for her key with icy cold fingers while her life's blood drained away, her mind became more and more fuddled. She tried to pierce the grey cotton wool to find someone else she could ask for help, or somewhere else she could go, or something else she could do. But she was unable to think of anyone, or any place, or anything.

Melvin was sitting in his favourite chair smoking his pipe. "Where the hell have you been?"

"In town for some messages. It's an awful night. I got soaked."

She went through to the kitchen to peel off her wet clothes and crouch gratefully over the fire.

The sight of Melvin had neverthless aroused resentment

in her. For years she had worked day and night as nanny, cook, cleaning woman, housekeeper, waitress, nurse, decorator, laundry maid and even shop assistant and book-keeper, because many a time she had helped Melvin fill in forms and do books for the bakery. On top of all this she had borne his children. And now at the end of all the years of slaving, what had she to show for it?

Melvin had the house in his name and he owned the furniture and everything in it. He had the business. He had the earning capacity.

It struck her that there was a wicked inequality in law, and in marriage, and in every sphere, between the sexes.

Anger burned feebly inside her. She tried to fan its flames but had not the strength. Every ounce of energy was needed to concentrate on making a meal and then afterwards to face the long night looking after old Duncan.

There was no use going to bed any more. No use undressing only to dress again; to go to bed and have to rise again, to drag herself to the old man's room to attend to him or perhaps to search for him outside, in the garden, or the crescent, or perhaps she might not hear him leave and he would wander further away.

After Melvin left for the bakehouse, Catriona just sat in a chair as if in a trance, waiting for her father-in-law to call. Her head nodded and jerked as sleep played hide and seek with her. Sometimes when she thought she heard him, she went out to the hall and stood hunched up in an agony of listening in the silent darkness.

All the time her head echoed with the wailing sound of her name.

*Catriona! Catriona! Catriona!*

Yet the hall was devoid of all sound except the nervous fluttering of her breathing.

At last she could bear the suspense no longer, and she dragged herself up the stairs to make sure that he was all right.

Immediately she went into his room and saw the old

face, hollow-cheeked and sagging-jawed against the pillow, she knew he was dead.

She leaned back against the wall, weak with relief. She admitted to herself she was glad he was dead. She could feel no guilt. She was beyond guilt or grief or caring.

But she said out loud:

"I'm sorry, Da."

Then she forced herself to put on her coat and go and tell Melvin.

Before she reached the bakery, however, the rain-shimmered streets lapped slowly away from her. She felt herself without bones, a piece of seaweed undulating with the tide until it gradually engulfed her.

Melvin did not discover until next morning that his father was dead and it was much later before he found she was in hospital.

By that time Catriona had been through an emergency operation and had her uterus and her ovaries removed.

"You were lucky!" the surgeon told her. "We got you just in time. Now with plenty of rest and care you should be all right."

Melvin was the first person she saw after she was back in bed and coming out of the anaesthetic.

She thought at first she was still out on the street, still in pain and still seeing Glasgow through a misty grey blue. Then Melvin's bulbous eyes, staring wildly, came into focus. He was waving a bunch of flowers in front of her face. She tried to move her head to escape from them.

"You're all right," she heard him shout excitedly. "I knew it! I knew you couldn't do this to me!"

Afterwards she wondered what he meant. Was it some sort of confession of faith in her? Or was it that he had been afraid she might die like his first wife and he could not bear any more guilt?

But why should he feel guilt?

In the safe world of the hospital, lying tucked neatly

in her white bed, drifting in and out of sleep, being con-
scientiously cared for by the hospital doctors and nurses,
she could take a more objective view of her husband.

Poor Melvin. Surely he was no more responsible for
harming his first wife than she was responsible for the
death of her baby.

When he came back to visit her she managed to thank
him for the flowers. He seemed pleased, and strolled
around the bed jingling coins in his pockets and assuring
her:

"Anything you need or want, just tell me."

She did not answer him. She only smiled then closed
her eyes and pretended to have fallen asleep.

She felt an instinct of quiet prudence taking root. Her
first need was to survive. Layers of caution enfolded her.
She drew them around like secrets she would never
divulge or share.

But she wrote to Madge and to Julie and let them know
that she was in hospital.

Madge said, "I told you, didn't I? Some people have
all the luck! Now you've had everything taken away and
you'll never be able to have any more weans!"

Melvin and the boys had been by her bedside when
Julie arrived bright and smart and talkative, yet with
restless eyes that kept straying to Melvin and the children.

Madge envied her the family she could not have and
Julie envied her the family she had. The next time they
came and left together, and before she went away Madge
said:

"Oh, by the way, you'll never guess who's coming around
our place now. Him and Alec are the best of pals."

"Who?"

"Sammy Hunter. Ruth's man. He knows about Alec
being with her that night as well."

"Fancy!"

"It makes you think, doesn't it?" Madge said. "Maybe
the big midden was telling me the truth after all!"

215

"Have I met this Sammy?" Julie asked.

"No, hen," Madge laughed. "But you're welcome to come to my place any night he's there. That'll be a laugh, eh? Me as a matchmaker!"

Julie rolled her eyes.

"I only made a perfectly casual remark."

Catriona smiled.

"He's nice, Julie. I like Sammy very much."

"Hey, you! Less of it!" Madge punched her in the arm. "Never you mind liking Sammy very much. You've got a man already." She winked at Julie. "Now that she can't be caught out there'll be no holding her back. Randy wee bugger!"

Catriona shook her head.

"Madge, you're terrible."

But she felt a little more cheerful, a little more reassured and a little stronger after their visit.

"It's terribly kind of both of you to come and see me like this," she told them earnestly. "It means a lot to me. You've no idea how I appreciate it."

Julie laughed and as if on an impulse came back to the bedside and dropped a quick kiss on her cheek.

"No need to look so serious, pal. It's a hard life, but if we keep working at it we'll survive!"

Madge strode back too and kissed her noisily on the brow. "You're a right silly wee midden, always have been!"

For a long time after they left, Catriona felt warmed by their affection and friendship. She felt strangely cheered by what Madge had been saying about Sammy, too. It occurred to her how fascinating it was that in such odd little unexpected ways one person could influence another. Everybody was like pebbles dropping into a pool, making ripples that went on and on, their effect widening and widening.

By deciding to behave in a certain way Sammy had influenced Madge, although he probably did not know it, and now he was indirectly influencing her in her hospital bed as she struggled to regain strength and purpose to face the world outside.

Suddenly she felt keenly and urgently aware of the importance of ordinary day-to-day human relationships. It seemed to her that every word everybody ever said, every attitude, every action, helped to swell the influence of either good or bad in the world. The fact that the pebbles could not see the ripples did not matter. There was no doubt at all that the ripples were there.

And if every casual word or deed to strangers had vital importance in the scheme of things, how much more valuable and meaningful were those of family and friends. Couldn't she influence, even in tiny ways, her mother and people beyond her mother? Couldn't she influence Melvin, and the children and their children, and into the future in wider and wider reaches without end? And if Madge and Julie could help and influence her in the most unconscious and unexpected ways—couldn't she sometime, in some way, do the same for them?

Catriona felt the journey towards understanding, the challenge of life beginning. She felt, thanks to Sammy, that she had managed to get herself on the right track.

It would be nice to see Sammy again. Friends were so important. Friends were the links in the lifeline to which she must cling.

Yet, at the same time, thinking of Sammy brought depression and memories of the air-raids and the deaths of neighbours and good friends and her own son.

Sadness spread out and encompassed all the other mothers' sons and all the other neighbours all over the world, the unknown hundreds, thousands and millions. She felt overwhelmed by the tragedy of war. And she was afraid of what tomorrow might bring. But she struggled with the fear and suddenly into her mind came the text:

"Sufficient unto the day the evil thereof."

It seemed a revelation. She had strength enough for one day.

She relaxed back against the pillow and a breeze from the open window made golden cobwebs of her hair.

Her steady gaze studied a bird floating free in the sky outside; small and delicate yet powerful; swooping and circling, climbing triumphantly, higher and higher.

Catriona smiled her secret smile to herself.

One day was all she needed.